PRAISE FOR

"A gold-medal debut for the ShibSibs! This fun, fast-paced mystery with two fierce new detectives will keep young readers turning the pages until the twisty end!"

—Elizabeth Eulberg, author of the Great Shelby Holmes series

"Maia and Alex Shibutani have created an exciting world that explores mystery, the travails of competition, and the loving support of family. An entertaining read for all generations."

—Bobby Hundreds, author of *This Is Not a T-Shirt*

"A fun, exciting adventure all across Tokyo. The Kudo Kids are lovable and daring, proving to be highly relatable heroes that kids will root for."

—Lyla Lee, author of *Mindy Kim and the Yummy Seaweed Business* **and** *I'll Be the One*

KUDO KIDS
THE MYSTERY OF THE MASKED MEDALIST

MAIA AND ALEX SHIBUTANI

WITH MICHELLE SCHUSTERMAN

ILLUSTRATED BY YAOYAO MA VAN AS

RAZORBILL

RAZORBILL

An imprint of Penguin Random House LLC, New York

First published in the United States of America by Razorbill,
an imprint of Penguin Random House LLC, 2020

Text copyright © 2020 by Maia Shibutani and Alex Shibutani
Illustrations copyright © 2020 by Yaoyao Ma Van As

Visit us online at penguinrandomhouse.com

LIBRARY OF CONGRESS CATALOGING-IN-PUBLICATION DATA IS AVAILABLE
ISBN 9780593113738

Printed in the United States of America

1 3 5 7 9 10 8 6 4 2

Design by Maria Fazio
Text set in New Baskerville ITC

This book is a work of fiction. Any references to historical
events, real people, or real places are used fictitiously.
Other names, characters, places, and events are products of
the author's imagination, and any resemblance to actual events
or places or persons, living or dead, is entirely coincidental.

NOTE TO READER: When using the internet, it's important to keep
yourself safe. Be sure to follow your parents' rules. Information like your name,
school, hometown, and any other personal facts should always be kept private.
Never speak with strangers online, and if you ever feel worried
or uncomfortable, ask a trusted adult for help right away.

Mom and Dad,
your unconditional support and unwavering
belief gave us the hope to dream and
the strength to forge our own path

CHAPTER ONE
ANDY

BZZT-BZZT.

Andy Kudo froze with a forkful of mashed potatoes halfway to his mouth. Glancing around the dinner table, he shifted slightly in his seat to get a better look at the phone resting in his lap. It was a text from Devon Perez, his best friend from school, but the screen went dark before Andy could read it.

Mika grabbed a chicken leg from the platter in the middle of the table. "I wonder what we'll be eating for dinner tomorrow in Tokyo," she said, waving the leg enthusiastically. "Probably not fried chicken, right, Dad?"

Slowly, Andy unlocked his phone with one hand. Near his feet, a pair of dark brown eyes gazed at him pleadingly. "Sorry, Lily," Andy whispered. "No people food." The white Maltese gave him a sweet doggie grin, pink tongue lolling.

"Why not?" Dad was saying, helping himself to more broccoli. "We might have *karaage*!"

"Kara-ah-geh," Mika repeated. "Is that Japanese for fried chicken?"

"Yup," Dad replied. "It's really popular in Japan. It's a specific type of deep-frying method—not exactly like tempura, but similar."

"Mmm, like the sweet potato tempura at that restaurant Aunt Kei loves," Mika said dreamily. "Those are sooo good . . ."

"I'm sure we can find sweet potato tempura in Tokyo," Dad said. "Veggie tempura, fish tempura . . ."

"Shrimp tempura," Mom chimed in as she reached for the salad dressing. "Squid, octopus—"

"Octopus!" Mika's brown eyes widened. "For real?"

"For real. And it's delicious. In fact . . ." Dad sat up straighter, and Andy smiled to himself as he opened his messages. A travel writer who specialized in food, Dad could talk about it for hours, if no one stopped him. But before he could launch into a lengthy speech about the deliciousness of octopus, Mom cleared her throat.

"Andy?"

Andy jumped at the sound of his name, and the phone slid off his lap, hitting the carpet with a muffled *thump.*

"What was that?" Mika ducked down to look under the table just as Andy leaned over. Her gaze landed on the phone. "Oooh . . . Ha! Busted."

Lily gave Andy's face a sympathetic kiss. Po, the

family's other white Maltese, sat next to Mika's chair, eyes fixed on Mika's hands. Andy was pretty sure his sister had slipped the puppy a piece of chicken. He raised an eyebrow, and she responded with a slightly mischievous grin. Andy was a year older than Mika, but his eleven-year-old sister was pretty good at doing sneaky stuff like that and getting away with it. Andy, on the other hand . . .

"Is someone breaking the no-phones-at-the-dinner-table rule?" Dad asked in a tone of mock horror.

Sighing, Andy grabbed his phone and straightened up. "Sorry," he said, handing it to Mom. "There's supposed to be an *OlympiFan* update before the opening ceremony starts. We're *finally* going to find out what the secret grand prize is!"

Mom slid his phone into the pocket of her jeans before reaching for her fork. "I thought you said that little game starts tomorrow?"

"Midnight in Tokyo," Andy replied immediately. "Eight o'clock tomorrow morning in LA!"

"And it's not *little*, Mom," Mika added. "There are like thousands of players registered!"

"All over the world," Andy continued. "The game supports a ton of languages. English, Japanese, Korean, Spanish, Italian, French—"

"Okay, I get the picture," Mom said, pushing her wire-rimmed glasses up her nose. "You guys are really excited about this game."

Andy was more than excited. He'd downloaded the *OlympiFan* app the previous week, and every time he opened it, all he saw were the Rules of Play and the Gallery, which wasn't open yet. No one had any idea what the secret grand prize might be, and Andy couldn't wait to find out.

"I hope you two are still planning on watching the events, though," Dad added.

"Uh, *yeah.*" Mika bounced excitedly in her chair, and Andy nodded enthusiastically in agreement. He couldn't believe that they were going to Tokyo for more than two weeks—and during the Olympic Games! Mom was the editor in chief of Compete, a popular sports website, and between her job and Dad's work as a freelance travel writer, the Kudo kids had gone on some pretty awesome vacations.

But this trip was special. The Kudos were Japanese American, and Andy couldn't wait to visit the country of his heritage for the first time. Dad had been on several press trips to Tokyo, and he'd helped Andy and Mika come up with a long list of sights they wanted to see and food they wanted to try. Andy had downloaded a language app to help him learn some useful phrases in Japanese. Between exploring a city he'd heard so much about and attending the Summer Olympics, Andy thought his vacation couldn't get any cooler.

And then the *OlympiFan* game happened.

Andy loved puzzles. A *lot*. And he was really, really good at them. He had dozens of puzzle apps on his phone: anagram solvers, logic grids, word games, and cryptic puzzles. His favorite was *S-Cape*, an escape-room game that had a seemingly endless number of rooms. Andy was currently on level sixty-one, which was the captain's cabin on a sinking ship. So far, he hadn't been able to solve the puzzles fast enough to escape the cabin before water came gushing in through the broken windows. He was getting closer, though, and Andy loved a good challenge.

But thanks to *OlympiFan*, Andy was about to take a break from all other games. Even *S-Cape*.

"What time is it?" he asked suddenly, glancing down at his lap even though his phone was gone. "Is the opening ceremony about to start? Can we turn the TV on?"

"We just started eating!" Mom took a big bite of chicken, as if to prove her point.

"Yeah, but we might miss the beginning!"

"Technically, we missed the whole thing." Dad blinked twice, his expression innocent, a sure sign he was making a Dad joke. "It started at about six this morning."

"Ha ha." Andy rolled his eyes. "You know what I mean."

"We'll miss the *broadcast*," Mika added. "Andy's right, it's about to start! Can we *please* have the TV on while we eat, just this once?"

"I don't think—" Dad began, but he stopped when Mika tilted her head back and drew a deep breath.

"PLEEEE-EEEEE-EEEEE-EEEEEZZZ!"

Lily's head jerked up in alarm, and Po skittered out from under the table and darted into the kitchen. Andy couldn't help but laugh. Dad had dubbed it Mika's "pitiful sheep bleating"—a startlingly loud sound that she only resorted to in the most desperate circumstances. It usually worked, too. Sure enough, Andy saw the corners of Dad's lips twitching.

"Fine, you can watch. But you have to finish your broccoli!"

Mom tried to hide her smile as Mika flew across the living room and grabbed the remote. A few seconds later, a shot of the Olympic Stadium filled the screen. Andy gazed at the enormous oval stadium set against the Tokyo skyline. In a little more than a day, he would actually *be* there.

Mika returned to her seat, and Mom took the remote from her.

"We've still got a few minutes before the ceremony actually starts," Mom said, muting the TV. "Tell me more about this game. How do you play?"

"It's an augmented reality game," Andy told her. "Remember *Pokémon GO*? Or that zombie game Aunt Kei tried to get you to play last summer?"

"Don't remind me," Mom said with a big shudder.

"We were at the grocery store, and I held my phone up and saw a zombie in the produce section. I screamed so loudly, this poor lady dropped a gigantic jar of pickles and it shattered all over the floor. I deleted that app from my phone right there."

Andy snickered, and so did Mika. Aunt Kei had told them that story at least a dozen times, but it never got any less funny.

"No zombies in this game," Mika said as Andy took another bite of chicken. "There are three virtual medals—Bronze, Silver, and Gold—and a bunch of clues, all hidden in different locations in Tokyo. Tomorrow the app will tell us where to go to find clues for the Bronze medal. The clues and the medals are all worth points you can use to download video interviews with Olympic athletes. There's also a secret grand prize that's super mysterious."

"No one even knows who designed the game," Andy added eagerly around a mouthful of food. "They're called—"

"Andy, no talking with your mouth full!" Mom gave him a stern look, and Andy chewed faster.

"Sorry," he said once he'd swallowed. "I'm just so excited—okay, so they're called the Masked Medalist." Andy took another giant bite of chicken despite Mom's protests. "They're a former Olympic athlete, and they have an Instagram account. But that's all anyone knows about them. Okay, sorry! I'm done." He took a long, loud slurp of water to wash down the chicken, and Mika giggled.

"All the posts they share on their Instagram account are photos and videos from past Olympic Games," Mika said. "It's so cool!"

"Players are supposed to form teams," Andy continued. "I think seven is the most people you can have on a team. Devon and Riley are on a team with us!"

Mika beamed and nodded. "Riley's so excited! She's been going to the library like every day this summer researching stuff about Tokyo."

"Riley goes to the library every day anyway," Andy pointed out. Riley Jenkins was Mika's best friend. Andy had never met anyone who read as much as she did. One time when he'd been walking Lily and Po, he'd spotted Riley across the street with her beagle, Turtle. Riley had Turtle's leash in one hand and a book in the other, and she was reading *while she walked*. Andy did that with his phone sometimes, but he'd never seen anyone walk around with her nose buried in a book. He figured it was a good thing Turtle was such a slow walker—after all, that's how he'd gotten his name.

Dad looked surprised. "Wait—how can Devon and Riley play if they're not in Tokyo?"

"Because the game has both AR and VR modes. Augmented reality and virtual reality," Andy added when his parents frowned in confusion. "Anyone can play in VR mode, no matter where they are."

"Ah, I get it." Dad paused. "Nope, I don't get it at all."

"Clues will be all around Tokyo," Mika explained. "Playing in AR mode in Tokyo means you can actually see them through your phone."

"And playing in VR mode is kind of like using a street view of Google Maps," Andy finished. "Virtual Tokyo."

Mom took a sip of iced tea and shook her head. "Remember when Game Boys first came out, Tom?"

"I thought *Tetris* was actual sorcery," Dad said, his voice completely deadpan.

"Literal magic," Mom agreed.

Mika's eyes twinkled. "What about microwaves? Did you think those were magic boxes?"

"How about light bulbs?" Andy adopted an innocent expression. "You guys were born before those were invented, right?"

"And forks," Mika added, tapping hers against her plate.

"And books."

"And pencils."

"And . . ." "And telephones!"

Mika giggled, and Dad let out a big sigh. "Ah, yes. When I was your age, we had nothing to read or write with.

We couldn't even text our friends all through dinner!"

"It's true," Mom said, smiling. "I'm not sure how we ever communicated with anyone!"

Andy rolled his eyes, and Mika slumped down in her chair, laughing. Dad opened his mouth to say something else, but then his gaze fell on the TV. "Is it starting?"

All four of them turned to the TV. The interior of the stadium was completely dark except for a few beams of light, which shone down from the ceiling like spotlights crisscrossing over the audience. The camera suddenly switched back to two commentators, and Mom glanced at her watch.

"We've still got a few minutes."

Andy shoveled down the rest of his potatoes, then stood and picked up his plate. "Um dun," he announced around the mouthful of food, and Mika shot to her feet, too.

"Thanks for dinner!" she said.

Mom eyed her plate. "Mika, broccoli? That was the deal. And, Andy, what did I just say about talking with food in your mouth?"

Andy made a show of swallowing as Mika crammed three spears of broccoli into her mouth.

"Mika!" Dad protested, but she was already marching into the kitchen, Andy right behind her. They rinsed their dishes, loaded them in the dishwasher, and then hurried into the living room. Mika grabbed her phone off the coffee table and flopped back onto the sofa.

Andy turned to face the dining room table, where Mom and Dad were stacking up the rest of the dishes. "Mom?"

"Yes, oh . . . right." Mom pulled his phone from her pocket and dropped it into his outstretched palm. "Enjoy your magic box."

Grinning, Andy hurried back to the sofa. Unlocking his phone, he opened his messages.

> **DP:** DID U SEE??

> **DP:** SECRET GRAND PRIZE

> **DP:** 😲😲😲😲😲

Andy felt his pulse quicken. He opened *OlympiFan* and read the Masked Medalist's post. As he read, his mouth fell open. He read it again as a commercial for a sportswear company replaced the commentators on TV.

" *. . . use #TeamWorld to enter. Enspire is a proud sponsor of the Olympic and Paralympic Games.* "

Mika's eyes were flicking back and forth between her phone and the TV. Andy could see an Instagram post on Mika's screen.

"Did they post about it there, too?" he asked eagerly. Mika let out a surprised squeak and hid the screen from him.

"What? I wasn't . . . What are you talking about?"

"The Masked Medalist's update!"

"Oh! Yeah. No. Um." Mika blinked. "Wait. There's an update?"

"Yes!" Andy read from his screen, his voice rising in his excitement. "'The team to correctly guess the Masked Medalist's identity will get to be *beta testers for my next games*!'"

He held his phone out and watched as his sister read the rest of the update, her expression rapidly changing from confused to ecstatic.

"Beta testers for new games?!" she yelped. "And working with an actual Olympian?! *Wow.* That would be so amazing!"

"You mean that *will* be so amazing," Andy corrected her with a grin. Opening his messages, he started typing a response to Devon. "We're def gonna win this thing."

Hello, OlympiFans! At long last, the Olympic Games are here—which means our game is finally about to begin. You'll find tons of awesome videos featuring your favorite Olympic athletes in the OlympiFan Gallery that officially opens tomorrow!

Only one team will win the **SECRET GRAND PRIZE** . . . but not with points. To win, your team must answer one question:

Who is the Masked Medalist?

That's right—the first team to correctly guess my identity will win the **SECRET GRAND PRIZE:** becoming *beta testers for my upcoming games*! I'm launching a new gaming company, so it's time for the Masked Medalist to be unmasked. Those three medals you're searching for come with more than points: each one includes a hint or two that will help your team guess who I am. Each team will have **ONE** chance to guess, so every hint helps! Teams who find medals can choose between more points, or more hints:

Bronze
250 points + 2 hints OR 500 points + 1 hint
The team who wins the Bronze will immediately receive the next 5 locations and a 1-hour head start on the search for the Silver medal!

Silver
500 points + 2 hints OR 750 points + 1 hint
The team who wins the Silver will immediately receive the last 5 locations and a 1-hour head start on the search for the Gold medal!

Gold
750 points + 2 hints OR 1,000 points + 1 hint

Are you ready? Set? . . .

GO!!!

CHAPTER TWO
MIKA

BEEP-BEEP. BEEP-BEEP.

Mika jolted upright in bed and snatched her phone from her nightstand. She swiped the screen, silencing the robot ringtone she'd selected for her alarm. The clock read 7:00 a.m., and Mika felt a thrill of excitement. This afternoon, she'd be on a plane to Tokyo!

Opening her notes app, Mika scanned the extensive checklist she'd made the previous week. Two bags—both blue, Mika's favorite color—sat next to her door: a large suitcase with wheels, and a matching backpack with extra straps that attached to the suitcase. She'd checked everything off her list last night as she packed before going to bed, but it couldn't hurt to go over it again, just to be safe.

A map on the dresser caught Mika's eye, and she grimaced. She and Riley had gone on a tour of Marshall Middle School with the rest of their fifth-grade class at the end of spring. The building had seemed like a gigantic maze of never-ending hallways with banging lockers, loud bells, and crowds of scary older kids moving from class to class. Mika had taken the map home, intent on memorizing it, but looking at it just made her even more nervous about starting sixth grade.

After brushing her teeth, pulling her long black hair into a ponytail, and changing into denim shorts and a blue-and-white-striped shirt, Mika headed downstairs. Her brother's door was closed, and Mika was pretty sure she could hear his alarm still going off inside. Mom had told them to get up at seven. For Mika, that meant setting an alarm for seven. For Andy, that meant setting an alarm for six thirty. Or at least, that's what Mika told him to do before they'd gone to bed.

"You have to actually *get up* at seven," she'd said anxiously. "If you sleep in, we'll miss our flight!"

"I won't sleep in," Andy had replied, rolling his eyes as he set his alarm for seven. "I promise."

Lily and Po, like two fluffy white tornadoes, greeted Mika at the foot of the stairs, dragging their leashes behind them. She knelt down to snuggle both of them and spotted Mom in the living room, rummaging through a small box.

"Plenty of food for the next few weeks, bowls, beds, two rubber bones . . ." Mom looked up at Mika. "Did I forget anything?"

"Nope!" Mika gave each puppy a kiss. "Have fun with Riley and Turtle, guys!"

"Be back in a few minutes." Mom held the box under one arm and picked up the leashes. She glanced up the stairs. "Is Andy awake yet?"

"His alarm's going off," Mika told her. "And I set a second one on his phone last night while he was in the shower. With a siren ringtone. I knew he'd sleep through the first one."

Mom laughed. "Nice job!"

When Mika entered the kitchen, she found Dad grinding coffee beans. "Morning!" he said cheerfully, pouring the grounds into the coffee maker. "How'd you sleep?"

"Pretty good," Mika replied. It wasn't exactly true. She'd been so excited about their trip that she'd stayed awake for hours. "What time are we leaving?"

"Quarter to eight-ish." Two pieces of toast popped up from the toaster. Whistling, Dad opened the fridge and pulled out the butter.

Mika grabbed a box of cereal from the pantry. As she poured herself a bowl, her phone buzzed in her pocket. She sat down at the table with the cereal and pulled her phone out.

> **RJ:** Did you do it?!?!

Mika's stomach did a little flip. She started to respond to Riley, but then Dad sat down at the table with his toast. Quickly, Mika closed the message and opened *OlympiFan* instead.

"Check it out," she said, setting her phone down so that Dad could see the screen. After the opening ceremony, *OlympiFan*'s Gallery had opened, and there were tons of videos, each featuring a different Olympic athlete—but they were all locked, and each one "cost" twenty points. Mika and Andy had sat on the couch for hours scrolling through all of the names until Mom finally convinced them to go to bed.

"Team MADR?" Dad's brow furrowed. "What's that?"

Mika grinned. "That's our team name. Mika-Andy-Devon-Riley."

"Ah."

"See, once you form a team you get a private chat room, which is cool because we won't have to keep texting each other. And you can look at other players' profiles and send them messages and pictures, too." Mika cast a sideways glance at Dad. "It's not that different from having an Instagram account, actually."

The coffee maker beeped, and Dad stood up. "Oh, really?"

"Really." Mika sat up straighter, watching as Dad poured a cup of coffee. "It's *practically* the same thing, if you really think about it. And you and Mom don't mind Andy and me playing *OlympiFan*, sooo . . ."

"Sooo . . ." Dad sat down again, cradling the mug in his hands. "Mika, it feels like we've had this conversation at least twice a week this summer. You know the rule—no social media until you're thirteen."

Mika slumped back down in her chair. "But it's the same thing!" she repeated.

"It's not the same thing," Dad said lightly. "*Olympi-Fan* is a game. You and Andy have lots of games on your phones, and most of them let you interact with other players. Social media is different."

"But—"

"Mika, you already know what Mom and I think about this." Dad took a sip of coffee. "What's going on? You didn't seem all that interested in Instagram until recently. Is it because of the masked . . . whatever?"

"The Masked Medalist," Mika said. "And no, that's not why. Their account is public, so I can see their posts. I just . . . I want my own account."

"Why?"

Mika shrugged, eating a spoonful of cereal to stall for time. The truth was that right after fifth-grade graduation, Riley had joined Instagram. She mostly posted pictures of Turtle and the books she was reading. But a bunch of other kids from school were on there too, and every time Mika went to look at Riley's pictures, she could read all of their comments. Then she'd look at *their* photos and see Riley's comments. It felt like there was a fun party going on without her— Mika didn't like it one bit.

And the night before, Mika had found another

reason to join Instagram. A *big* one. But she definitely couldn't tell Dad about that.

She could tell Riley, though. Mika was itching to text her best friend back, but Dad was still watching her.

"My photos are really good," she said finally. "You and Mom always say that."

"They *are* really good," Dad agreed. "You have a photographer's eye."

Mika felt a rush of happiness at the praise. "And, well, I could share them on Instagram."

"You could." Dad smiled. "And you will! When you're thirteen. Okay?"

"Okay." Mika's stomach twisted with guilt. She took another bite of cereal and tried to ignore it.

"Morning!" Mom breezed into the kitchen, heading straight for the coffee maker. "I just scheduled a car. It'll be here in about twenty minutes. Mika, would you see if Andy needs any help packing when you're done with that?"

"Sure!"

Mika finished off her cereal, washed out the bowl, and raced up the stairs two at a time. "Knock-knock!" she called before barreling into Andy's room. "Are you ready to—*uh-oh*."

Andy was sprawled on top of his comforter, fast asleep, his phone clutched in one hand. He let out a soft snore, and Mika snickered.

"Come *onnn*. I know you're faking."

But Andy didn't budge. Mika frowned.

"Are you seriously still asleep?! What about the second alarm?"

She marched over to his bed and snatched the phone from his hand.

"Wha—" Andy blinked blearily, then tried to grab the phone back. Mika held it out of reach and tapped the screen, but it remained dark.

"Your battery died, you dork!" she exclaimed. "Why didn't you plug it in before you went to bed?"

"I meant to." Andy sat up, rubbing his eyes. "I don't even remember falling asleep."

Mika saw the charger sticking out from under his bed. She grabbed it and plugged it in, then set his phone down on the dresser to charge. "We're leaving in twenty minutes," she told him. "Want me to take your bags downstairs while you get dressed?"

"Ummm . . ." A guilty expression flashed across her brother's face, and she followed his gaze to the yellow suitcase lying open by the door. Other than a few pairs of shorts, it was empty.

"Andy!" Mika cried. "You aren't even *packed* yet?"

"I started to!" he said defensively, jumping out of bed and running over to his closet. "But then I started looking at the map of Tokyo in *OlympiFan*, and, well . . ."

Mika groaned. Pulling out her own phone, she opened the checklist again. "Okay. You pack your clothes, I'll go get your stuff from the bathroom."

"Thanks!" Andy yelled, already pulling shirts off their hangers.

Fifteen minutes later, Mika dragged Andy's stuffed suitcase down the stairs. Through the window next to the front door, she saw a silver minivan pulling up to the curb. "The car's here!" she bellowed.

Mika helped Mom and Dad load all of their luggage into the trunk, checking over her shoulder every few seconds for Andy. Finally, he burst outside and jogged down the sidewalk, struggling to zip up his bag. Mom locked the front door while Mika and Andy climbed into the back seat. Dad greeted the driver and slid into the passenger seat in front of Mika. Once Mom was buckled in, they were off.

Exhaling, Mika checked the time on her phone. Seven forty-eight. Still plenty of time to make their flight, even if the line at security was superlong.

Andy yawned widely. "Thanks for helping me pack," he said. "Ugh, I'm starving."

"Told ya. Should've woken up earlier." Mika unzipped the front pocket of the backpack at her feet. "Luckily you have a really awesome and brilliant sister."

She handed him a granola bar, and Andy grinned, taking it. "I *do* have an awesome sister."

"You forgot brilliant."

"No I didn't."

Mika elbowed him, and he nudged her away before unwrapping the granola bar. While he ate, Mika opened her messages again. Riley had sent another text:

RJ: WELL???

But before Mika could type a response, Andy started shifting around in his seat. His eyes were wide and frantic as he patted his pockets, then unzipped his backpack. The minivan headed up the ramp onto the highway. Palm trees streamed past against a clear blue sky.

"Oh no," Andy mumbled. "No no no no no no . . ."

"Forget something?" Dad asked, twisting around in his seat.

"Probably, considering he packed like ten minutes ago," Mika said teasingly. But Andy was too busy rummaging through the jumbled-up contents of his backpack to answer.

"It's okay, Andy," Mom told him. "Whatever you forgot, we'll be able to find it in Tokyo."

Andy set his backpack on the floor, then checked his pockets again. "Um, I don't think so."

"What'd you forget?" Dad asked.

Andy swallowed. "My phone. The battery died, so I was letting it charge until the last minute, but then the car showed up and . . ."

Groaning, Mika thunked her head against her seat. "Andy!"

Mom and Dad exchanged a look. "All right, he wins." Mom was trying to sound easygoing, but her smile was tight. "We definitely can't find Andy's phone in Tokyo."

The driver glanced at Dad. "Am I turning around?"

"I'm afraid so," Dad replied.

Mika fought down a small wave of panic as the minivan moved into the right lane to exit.

"We've got time, it's okay," Mom said, checking her watch. "Everybody relax."

But thanks to a few ridiculously long red lights, it was almost fifteen minutes before they pulled up in front of the house. As Mom and Andy hustled out of the minivan and ran up the sidewalk, Mika turned her attention back to her phone. She opened the messages app and typed a quick response to Riley.

> **MK:** Not yet, but I'm going to! 🎭

She hit send, then felt a wave of excitement—and guilt, too. Mika wasn't a rule breaker. Well, not of the important rules, the *big* ones. But this was different.

Besides, wasn't a girl entitled to have a secret or two?

OLYMPIFAN UPDATE!
Locations for the Bronze Medal

Good morning/afternoon/evening, OlympiFans!
Thousands of the greatest athletes in the world are in Tokyo right now, getting ready to rock their events. Are **YOU** as ready as they are? Because, here we go ... clues leading to the virtual Bronze medal are waiting for you in these locations:

Shibuya

Shinjuku

Harajuku

Jingumae

Aoyama

Happy clue hunting, OlympiFans!

CHAPTER THREE
ANDY

"WE'RE NEVER GONNA make it."

Andy didn't respond to his sister, who was standing on tiptoe trying to see how many people were still ahead of them in the security check line. He glanced from his mom to his dad. They both looked calm, but in that forced way adults had when they didn't want you to know they were worried.

He couldn't believe he'd left his phone at home. Or that he'd slept in. Well, Andy admitted to himself, maybe that part wasn't so surprising. Especially considering he'd been up really late on *OlympiFan*. There was a map of Tokyo, and tapping on a spot brought up a description of the area with some of the most popular attractions. Andy had read them until drifting off to sleep . . . without charging his phone. Now, thanks to him—and a few ridiculously slow red lights, and traffic on the highway, and a long wait at baggage check, and just a ton of bad luck in general—the Kudos might miss their flight to Tokyo.

The line moved forward, and Dad checked the time on his phone. "Boarding starts in five minutes," he said, and Andy's stomach plummeted. "That usually takes at least half an hour," Dad added reassuringly.

"We'll make it," Mom agreed, probably because Mika was clawing at her cheeks with her fingers in a way that made her look slightly bug-eyed. "Relax, okay?"

Mika nodded, but she kept pulling at her face. Andy would've laughed if he hadn't felt so guilty.

"Here we go," Dad said as the line moved again. "Shoes off!"

Andy moved quickly, placing his sneakers and phone in a bin, then slid it down the conveyor belt along with his backpack. He went through the body scanner first, followed by Mika, and they scrambled to get their shoes back on while Mom and Dad came through.

"All right," Dad said, hoisting the strap of his laptop bag over his shoulder. "Shoes, bags, phones—everyone got everything? *Andy?*"

"Yeah, I have everything," Andy mumbled, grabbing his phone from the bin.

Mom checked her watch. "Okay, it's only been boarding for a few minutes. Gate C54 . . ." She squinted at the signs overhead, and her expression tightened. "Ah."

Andy followed her gaze and saw the nearest gate was C3. "C54?" he said with a groan. "It's sooo far!"

Dad had already started jogging through the terminal. "Well, let's get a move on!"

He led the way, with Andy and Mika racing to keep up with him and Mom following to make sure they didn't get separated as they dodged around groups of travelers. Andy counted the gates as they flew past each one. By C24, he had a stitch in his side. Next to him, Mika's face shone with sweat. When they passed C49, Andy heard an announcement over the intercom.

"This is the last call for passengers boarding flight 7015 to Tokyo."

"That's us!" Dad put on a burst of speed, and Mika let out a sound that was half laugh, half yelp. Andy felt laughter bubbling up in his throat, too. They'd never come this close to missing a flight before. He couldn't wait to text Devon and tell him about it once he was on the plane. *If* he got on the plane.

At last, the sign reading C54 came into view. Andy spotted a gate agent moving to close the door, and his heart stuttered in his chest.

"We're here!" Dad yelled so loudly that several people turned to stare at him. "Wait, hold the door!"

The woman looked slightly amused as the Kudos sprinted toward her. Smiling, she gestured to the ticket scanner.

"Don't worry, you made it!"

Andy came to a halt, gasping for air. He opened the

app with his plane ticket and held his phone over the scanner, then followed Dad onto the jet bridge. When they reached the plane, a few passengers stood just outside, still waiting to board. Mika and Mom joined them, both breathing heavily.

Mom took off her glasses and wiped her forehead on her sleeve. "Well, that was some morning workout."

"Maybe we should race at the Olympics," Andy said, grinning. "I bet we could win a medal for track!"

Mika rolled her eyes, but she was still too out of breath to say anything.

A few minutes later, Andy had stowed his and Mika's backpacks in the overhead compartment, closed the latch, and flopped down in the aisle seat. "I swear I'll never sleep in again."

Mika snorted, not taking her eyes off her phone. "Yeah, right." But she didn't sound mad anymore.

"You two okay?" Mom's face appeared over the seats in front of them, and Mika jumped and slapped her phone facedown on her legs. Andy glanced at her but didn't say anything.

"Yup!" Andy tapped at the screen on the back of Mom's seat, scrolling through the movies. "I'm gonna find something to watch."

Mom smiled and turned around to face the front again. As soon as she did, Andy nudged Mika's arm.

"Okay, what's going on?"

Mika gave him a look of false innocence that Andy knew all too well. "Nothing!"

"You hid your phone from Mom. Why?"

Sighing, Mika turned her phone over so Andy could see the screen. It was a photo of a little boy running toward an older woman. Probably his grandmother, Andy thought, leaning closer to get a better look. Her wrinkled face was lit up with a delighted smile, and her arms were outstretched. Andy recognized an airline sign in the background and glanced at Mika in surprise.

"Who are they? Did you take that this morning?"

"Yeah, when we were in that line to check our bags." Mika held the phone up and studied the photo. "I saw this kid with his parents, and he was so excited—he kept asking them over and over where Grandma was. Then she finally came down the escalator and his mom almost dropped him because he was squirming so much. His grandma looked so happy when she saw him running toward her, too . . . I don't know, I thought it would be a cool picture."

"It is." Andy couldn't help admiring his sister's photography skills. Mika had a knack for capturing pictures at the exact right moment. He noticed a few icons at the bottom of the screen and pointed. "What's all that?"

"I, um, downloaded a photo-editing app. I'm just

messing with the contrast and stuff. It's fun."

Frowning, Andy lowered his voice. "But why didn't you want Mom to see?"

Mika didn't take her eyes off her screen, but blinked rapidly. "Oh. Uh. I wanted to show her the final version, after it's all edited."

She was definitely lying. Or at least, not telling the whole truth. But Andy knew better than to push his sister—she'd tell him when she was ready. Shrugging, he pulled his phone out and opened *OlympiFan*, navigating to their team chat room.

> **Devon:** CLUES!!!

> **Riley:** AHHH! But Andy and Mika are at the airport!

> **Devon:** Should we start without them?

> **Riley:** I guess so??? 😕

> **Devon:** Andy I hope your plane has Wi-Fi!

"Mika!" Andy cried, much louder than he'd intended. In the rush to get to the airport, Andy had managed to forget that the clue locations for the Bronze medal would be revealed this morning! Startled, Mika looked up as Andy waved his phone at her. *"Clues!"*

"What?!" Mika hurriedly closed her photo and opened *OlympiFan* just as the plane began to move.

"Ladies and gentlemen, welcome aboard flight 7015 to Tokyo, Japan. Our flight time today is eleven hours and forty-five minutes . . ."

Mika groaned. "We have to switch our phones to airplane mode."

Andy looked around, his gaze falling on the Wi-Fi symbol near the light over Mom's head. "Aha!" Quickly, he typed a response to Devon and Riley.

> **Andy:** We're about to take off but there's Wi-Fi so we can play during the flight! BRB!

> **Andy:** We almost missed our flight 0_0

After sending the message, Andy put his phone on airplane mode. Adrenaline had already been coursing through him thanks to the race at the airport and the fear that they'd miss their flight. Knowing that *Olympi-Fan* had officially started—that other teams were collecting clues *right now* while Andy just sat here—was making him feel extra hyper. Like maybe he could run down the whole length of the terminal again.

At last, the plane took off, and Andy and Mika watched through the window as Los Angeles spread out below them. Once the view was nothing but blue sky and a few white, fluffy clouds, Mika went back to editing her photo. Andy scrolled through the movie selection again, although he had no intention of watching anything.

After a few minutes, the seat belt light flicked off just as the Wi-Fi symbol blinked on.

"Yes!"

Andy and Mika handed their phones to Mom, who used her work subscription to connect them. "Thanks!" Andy said eagerly, opening *OlympiFan* again.

Devon: You slept in, didn't you? 😄

Riley: I FOUND ONE! It was right outside a bookstore! 😎

Riley: Two more! Wow, there must be hundreds of clues. FYI, blue footprints mean you're far, yellow means getting warmer, pink means you're close.

Devon: Just added one!

Devon: Huh, the clues are just colors . . .

Andy had no idea what Riley meant by footprints or the clues being colors. He closed the messages and opened their team's clue collection. A white background filled his screen, with four small squares of color in the top left corner—one gray and three slightly different shades of red. A second later, a fifth square appeared, this one deep blue.

"What's it mean?" Mika asked, and Andy saw she had the clue collection open on her phone, too.

"I have no idea," he said, feeling another surge of

adrenaline. This puzzle wasn't going to be easy to solve—and that was exactly how Andy liked it.

Andy and Mika opened VR mode and examined the map. The five locations for the Bronze medal were all highlighted. They quickly decided on Aoyama as their first location, since it was pretty far from their hotel. Part of their strategy was to only pick places in VR mode that they wouldn't be able to visit for real when they played AR mode.

A street lined with fancy-looking shops and cafés filled Andy's screen, along with two tiny blue footprints at the bottom. He used the arrows in the middle of the screen to move down the street. After a minute or so, the footprints lightened to yellow.

"I think I'm close to one!" Andy told Mika, navigating toward a sushi restaurant. The footprints glowed pink, and then Andy spotted it—a tiny animated flag fluttering near the entrance. He tapped it, and as it zoomed toward him, he saw it was striped in orange, white, and green. A message appeared on the flag:

Player: AndyK
Team MADR (4)
Player clue total: 1
Team clue total: 6
Team ranking: 227

Suddenly it vanished, and Andy saw the sushi restaurant again, but the flag was gone.

"I got one, too!" Mika exclaimed. "We're up to seven!"

They continued to play for the next few hours, only pausing when the flight attendants stopped next to Andy to offer drinks and snacks, and then later for a bathroom break. Mika dozed off eventually, and Devon and Riley both exited the game after a while, but Andy couldn't stop playing. When he opened the scoreboard, Team MADR ranked fifty-second out of more than five hundred teams—but even as he looked at the numbers, the order shuffled again and his team dropped to seventy-ninth.

Of course, that ranking was only about the number of clues each team collected. Andy was hoping he could solve the puzzle and figure out where the Bronze medal was hidden without actually collecting every single clue. He'd noticed that each time another clue was added, the colorful squares shifted their order slightly.

He returned to exploring Aoyama. Occasionally, a bubble would pop up with a "fun fact" about the area. Reading them slowed Andy's search down a little bit, but he didn't mind.

When the flight attendants came by with meal options, Andy temporarily stopped playing to request a sandwich.

"Anything for your sister?" the attendant asked, gesturing to Mika, who was sound asleep.

Andy glanced at her. "Hey, Mika?" he said, poking

her arm. "Mika!" But she just mumbled something under her breath and shifted over to face the window. The flight attendant chuckled.

"I guess not."

After polishing off his sandwich, Andy went back to playing. It wasn't long before his eyelids began to droop, and he couldn't seem to stop yawning. *One more clue,* he told himself, navigating down another street lined with shops. *Or maybe two more . . .*

Hours later, Andy rubbed his eyes blearily. The cabin was totally dark and silent; other than a guy watching a superhero movie across the aisle, everyone Andy could see was asleep. Shifting to a more comfortable position, Andy dozed off again.

The next time he woke up, he could see sunlight peeking underneath the bottom of the window shade next to Mika. He checked the time on his phone: it was 9:34 p.m. in Los Angeles, but he had no idea what time zone they were in now.

Leaning out into the aisle, Andy spotted the flight attendants with the cart. The smell of food filled the air, and his stomach rumbled in response. Andy glanced at Mika again, but she was still completely out.

When the cart reached him, Andy accepted a turkey wrap with fruit. He played *OlympiFan* as he ate—Team MADR was up to eighty-eight clues now! Andy had just popped the last bite of the wrap into his mouth when the intercom pinged. A soothing voice spoke first in Japanese before translating into English.

"Ladies and gentlemen, in thirty minutes we will begin our descent into Narita International Airport."

Andy managed to grab four more clues before the Wi-Fi service ended. Carefully, he reached over Mika to slide the shade up, squinting against the bright light. Far below, he could just make out the tops of buildings, green patches of grass, and a winding river. Mesmerized, Andy gazed out the window as Tokyo grew closer and closer, and then the plane touched down with a slight lurch, speeding along the runway. As it slowed, Andy shifted excitedly in his chair.

"Grrr—GRRR—grrrrrrrrgle."

Andy looked at his sister, whose eyes were fluttering open.

"What was that noise?" Mika mumbled, shading her eyes from the sunlight.

"I'm pretty sure it was your stomach growling."

"Oh." Mika sat up straight and stared down the aisle. "I didn't miss dinner, did I?"

"You did," Andy told her, grinning. "And you missed another meal, too."

"What?!" Mika cried, clutching her stomach. "But I'm starving! How did I miss *two meals?*"

"Because you slept through the whole flight." Andy pointed out the window. "We're here."

1st		Majestic Turmoil	204
2nd		GhostCadets	198
3rd		夢	196
4th		ALLEYOOP	188
5th		SuperFan	187
6th		Dragonflame	182
7th		геймеров	180
8th		Cryptic	178
9th		EspectroRojo	176
10th		TheOracles	173

CHAPTER FOUR
MIKA

MIKA'S STOMACH GROWLED so loudly that the driver of their taxi caught her eye in the rearview mirror and chuckled. He said something in rapid Japanese, rubbing his belly exaggeratedly.

Mika didn't catch the phrase, but the meaning was obvious. "I'm *starving,*" she told him, trying to remember the phrase from her Japanese language app. "*Onaka sw* . . . um . . ."

"*Onaka suita,*" Dad supplied, taking out his wallet as the taxi pulled up in front of a towering hotel.

"*Onaka suita,* because *some*one let me sleep through two entire meals." Mika elbowed Andy, who rolled his eyes.

"I told you, I tried to wake you up! It's not my fault." Andy reached for his door, but it opened on its own. The driver grinned at Andy's surprise.

"Automatic," he said, and Andy grinned back.

"Whoa! Cool!"

Mika followed Andy out of the taxi. "What do you mean it's not your fault? You're the one who—whoa!"

Quickly, Andy pulled Mika out of the way just as a group of whooping, cheering teenagers went charging by. Mika stared at them, too startled to even think about taking a picture. They were all wearing matching T-shirts and fuzzy, super-tall top hats in different colors and patterns. A few held their phones up as they ran down the street, capturing their own madness on video.

"What's with those hats?"

Mom joined them, brushing her short bangs from her eyes. "I think they're flags! See? There's Japan, Russia, Brazil, USA, Germany . . ."

Mika spotted a red-and-white-striped hat, its blue brim covered in sparkly stars. "Oooh, I'm *so* getting one of those—uh-oh!"

The girl wearing the American flag hat cried out as a breeze lifted it right off her head. The hat tumbled down the sidewalk, and Mika hurried forward to scoop it up.

Beaming, the girl jogged toward Mika. *"Arigato!"*

"You're welcome," Mika said, handing her the hat.

The girl grinned. "Oh, you speak English?" Her words were thick with an accent Mika couldn't place.

"Yup!" Mika replied. "Hey, where'd you get—"

"You're OlympiFans!" Andy said suddenly. He pointed to the girl's T-shirt, which had TEAM SUPERFAN emblazoned in purple, with TOKYO INTERNATIONAL HIGH SCHOOL below in smaller print.

The girl's smile widened. "Yes! *OlympiFan* is our summer vacation assignment . . . to encourage team-building skills and learn more about Tokyo. Best homework ever!" she added, and Mika laughed. "Are you playing, too?"

"Yes! We haven't tried AR mode yet, though," Andy said.

"It's *so* fun," the girl said eagerly. "My name is Sabine, by the way—my player name is SabineTheGreat!"

"I'm Mika, and this is my brother, Andy," Mika replied, already opening the *OlympiFan* app on her phone. Next to her, Andy did the same. "Team SuperFan, SabineTheGreat . . . there! Just sent a friend request."

"Cool!" Sabine tapped her screen, and Mika saw her own profile appear. "Oh wow, you're from LA?"

"Sabine!" Down the street, a boy wearing a Japanese flag hat and enormous sunglasses waved his arms. "Hurry up!"

"Coming!" Sabine hollered back, then gave Mika and Andy another smile. "Nice to meet you guys. Good luck!"

"Good luck to you, too!" Mika called as Sabine ran off to rejoin her teammates. A few of them were Japanese, but others, like Sabine, were clearly not from Japan. Mika tried to imagine moving halfway across the world to attend an international high school. Starting middle school in her hometown was scary enough!

"I can't believe they get to play *OlympiFan* for school," she said. "I wonder how many clues they've found. We're probably so far behind!"

"Not that behind," Andy told her as they walked back over to Mom and Dad. "Our team had almost ninety clues by the time we landed."

"What?" Mika gawked at him. "Did you literally play the entire flight?"

"Well, yeah."

Mika was impressed, but Mom and Dad exchanged a look.

"I hope you two are still planning on exploring Tokyo," Mom said wryly. "We didn't come all this way for you to be on your phones the whole time."

"But that's what's so great about *OlympiFan*." Andy grabbed his suitcase, and he and Mika followed their parents into the hotel. "Sightseeing is a part of it, because you have to visit all these different places to find all the clues, and—"

"Karen Kudo!"

Andy fell quiet as he and Mika stared at the young man hurrying toward Mom. He had cropped black curls, brown skin, and a broad smile that Mika recognized instantly.

"Oh my god, that's Wesley Brooks!" she whispered to Andy, whose eyes widened in recognition. Mika vividly remembered seeing replays of Wesley's near-flawless gymnastics performances in the 2012 Olympics, where he'd won two silver medals. Plus, he was really charming in his interviews.

"So great to finally meet you in person," Wesley was saying as he shook Mom's hand. "Hana and I are thrilled to be working with Compete during the Games."

"I'm really glad to have you both on board," Mom said, returning his smile. "Wesley, this is my husband, Tom, and our kids, Andy and Mika."

Mika felt her face turn red as Wesley aimed his dazzling smile at her.

"Good to meet you all," he said, shaking Dad's hand enthusiastically, then Andy's, then Mika's. She managed a small squeak in response, already mentally composing a text to Riley about this. "Oh, here's Hana!"

He stepped to the side and gestured to a woman hurrying across the lobby, black ponytail swinging with every step. Mika thought she looked vaguely familiar, too. Was she another Olympic athlete?

"Hana Takahashi, this is Karen Kudo from Compete." Wesley made the introductions this time. When he got to Mika, he must have caught the questioning look on her face, because he leaned down and added in a stage whisper: "Swimmer, Team Japan."

Hana arched an eyebrow. "So you recognized Wesley, but not me?" she teased, a light accent rounding her words.

Mika felt her face flame up again. "I, um, well, I've seen him online . . ."

But Hana was laughing. "It's okay. I'm not obsessed with social media like Wesley is."

"I'm not *obsessed*," Wesley argued good-naturedly. "I'm *accessible*. I don't think this one has ever tweeted," he added to Mom. "If we're going to be covering the Games on Compete's social media accounts, you and I might have to teach her a few things—like what Instagram even *is*."

Hana scrunched her nose. "That's the one with the pictures, right?" Her expression made it clear that she was joking, and everyone laughed. Mika's heart gave an extra-hard *thump* as she thought of the apps she'd downloaded before their flight—the photo-editing one, and the other one. The one Andy hadn't seen.

"I'm sure you'll figure it out," Mom told Hana with a grin.

"Oh, don't worry," Hana said, returning the smile. "I might not tweet, but that doesn't mean I'm not tech savvy. So we have a meeting in about half an hour, right? Six o'clock?"

Mom nodded. "That's right—the conference room on the third floor. I'll see you both there?"

"Absolutely!" Wesley gave them a cheery wave, and Hana nodded and smiled. Mika still felt a little starstruck as she and Andy followed their parents to the reception desk. While Mom and Dad checked in, she opened the browser on her phone. A moment later, she nudged Andy.

"Hana won *two* gold medals in London!" Mika whispered, showing him the article she'd found. "In the freestyle and the butterfly races. And she's so nice! Wesley, too!"

Andy looked amused. "Did you think they'd be snobby or something?"

"I don't know! I've never met anyone famous before."

"Room keys!" Mom turned around, handing Andy and Mika each a card. "We're in suite 406."

"Ooh, a suite?" Mika asked excitedly. "I didn't know you were going to get all fancy."

Mom smiled. "Not so much 'fancy' as getting separate rooms so you guys don't have to deal with Dad's snoring."

Giggling, Mika grabbed her suitcase and headed toward the elevators with her family. For the first time, she took a good look around the lobby. A pretty marble fountain stood in the middle, and trees with wide branches and thick green leaves seemed to grow right out of the glittering gray marble tiles. An escalator led up to the second floor, its rails glowing blue, then green, then yellow. Mika caught a glimpse of a café, some restaurants, and a few small shops on the second floor before the elevator doors slid shut.

"What's that, Dad?" Andy asked. Mika turned to see Dad studying a small piece of paper.

"Someone left a message with the concierge asking

me to call as soon as I arrived," Dad said, brow furrowed. "A woman named Emi Suzuki. I know I've heard that name before, but I can't place it."

Ping! The doors slid open, and they headed down the hall to room 406, where Mom scanned her key card. Mika followed her inside eagerly. The rooms weren't very big, but really nice—one with two twin beds for Andy and Mika, and another one with a big bed, plus a desk and a window with a nice view of the bustling street below.

Mika tossed her backpack onto a twin bed, then flipped the switch on one of the lamps. Nothing. Frowning, she tried the other lamp, then joined her parents in their room.

Dad was already on the phone, so Mika kept her voice low. "I don't think the lights work!"

Mom glanced up and smiled. "Oh, right—the receptionist mentioned this. Check it out!"

Mika and Andy watched as Mom slid her key card into an electric holder next to the door. The overhead lights came on, and through the doorway to her and Andy's room, Mika saw the two lamps come on as well.

"It's eco-friendly!" Mom explained, leaving her card in the holder and returning to unpacking her suitcase. "When you leave the room, you take your key card out and all of the lights turn off. Big energy saver!"

"That's really cool!" Mika's eyes fell on the minifridge, and her stomach growled louder than ever. She hurried over to check the contents, then groaned. "Empty. Mom, do we have time to get something to eat before your meeting? I know you said we have a dinner reservation at eight, but that's almost two whole *hours* from now."

"Dad will take you guys to get something to eat as soon as he's off the phone," Mom replied, glancing over at Dad. "I'm going to be pretty busy working this whole trip, but lucky for you guys, your dad's a great tour guide."

"Absolutely, yes!" Dad's voice rose, and the three of them glanced over at him. He was nodding and jotting something down on the little pad of paper next to the phone. "Right . . . right. I'll be there in twenty minutes. Thanks again!" He hung up and turned to the others, his face filled with excitement. "Emi Suzuki is a publicist I met years ago on a press trip to Singapore," he said, adjusting his glasses. "She's working for Chef Kenji Abe. He's opening a new restaurant next week here in Tokyo, and Emi wants me to write a profile of him *and* review opening night!"

Mom's eyes widened. "Oh, I think I've heard of Kenji . . . Wasn't he on one of those cooking competition shows? *Kitchen Crashers,* or something like that?"

"Yup," Dad confirmed. "He's already a celebrity here. And he's notoriously private—Emi actually sounded kind of frustrated with how much he dislikes publicity. Apparently he's just very shy. But he knows he needs press for this opening, and Emi heard I was in town for the Olympics because . . ." Dad trailed off, blinking at Mom. "Because my wife is covering the Games. And we brought our kids. Um. I probably shouldn't have agreed to run over there without talking it over with you guys first."

Mika couldn't help but giggle, and Mom shook her head. "It's a fantastic opportunity," she said. "You should absolutely go. Andy and Mika can come to the meeting with me, and—"

"Or we can just go to the restaurant with Dad! I can totally review his food." Mika's stomach rumbled yet again, and she pointed to it. "See? I'm ready!"

Dad smiled, although he was running his fingers through his hair the way he did when he was stressed out. "The restaurant isn't open yet, honey. This is just an introductory meeting for us to chat about the angle of the profile I'd be writing—he's taking a break from testing recipes, and Emi said this is the only time he has to meet."

"There's probably someplace to eat close to the restaurant," Andy pointed out. "Mika and I could hang out there during your meeting."

"True, but that's just tonight," Dad said. "If Mom and I are both working this whole trip, what will you two do?"

"Play *OlympiFan*," Andy said immediately. "Explore Tokyo. Just like we planned!"

"You've let us go out on our own before!" Mika added, instantly warming to the idea. "Like in San Francisco, remember? We toured that chocolate factory by ourselves. And last summer in Seattle, Andy and I spent the whole morning on the waterfront while you interviewed that soccer player!"

Mom leaned against the desk and crossed her arms. "True . . . but this is a little different. It sounds like Dad will be super busy with this chef, and my schedule is packed. Tokyo is a really safe city, but you two have never been here before. You could easily get lost."

"Not with these." Andy waved his phone triumphantly. "And we can share our locations, so you can see wherever we are all the time!"

He swiped his phone open, and Mika immediately followed suit. A moment later, they held their screens out for their parents to see the map with their blue dots at the hotel. Dad glanced at Mom, and Mika held her breath.

"Please?" Andy asked.

Mom exhaled. "Okay. But first, we need to go over some ground rules."

Twenty minutes later, Andy and Mika hopped out of a taxi and waited for Dad to pay the driver. Mika gazed up at the buildings towering overhead, turning in a circle before examining the one they'd stopped in front of. The sun was starting to set, pink and orange light reflecting off the steel-and-glass building.

"Doesn't look like a restaurant," she said when Dad joined them.

"It's on the top floor." Dad gave Andy a pointed look. "Are you sure you have everything?"

Andy looked confused for a moment. Then he rolled his eyes. "Yes, I've got my phone *and* my portable charger."

"Me too!" Mika chimed in.

"And you have the name and address of our hotel in your phones?"

"Yes!" Andy said.

"Perfect." Dad glanced at his watch. "Okay. Meet back here in forty-five minutes, and stay on this block. Be safe, and have fun!"

"Thanks, Dad!" Mika gave him a quick hug, and Andy waved as Dad headed inside. Then Andy turned to Mika, and his wide grin mirrored her own.

"We're free!" she yelled, pumping her fist in the air. "For almost an hour, anyway."

Brightly colored advertisements covered the first few floors of the buildings, and even more banners hung higher up. Shoppers bustled around them, and Mika spotted more than a few Olympic T-shirts and hats. She wondered how many tourists visited a city just to attend the Olympics.

Andy already had his phone out and *OlympiFan* open. "Which way should we go first?" he said excitedly. "I already messaged Devon and Riley which area we're playing in."

Mika clutched her stomach. "I'm going in the direction of *food*," she informed him. "Nose, be my guide!" She turned and marched down the sidewalk, sniffing the air like Lily and Po did when she opened a can of dog food. Andy followed her, holding his phone out. Mika could see the blue footprints on the bottom of his screen as they drew closer to the intersection.

"Aha!" she cried, pointing.

Andy looked up. "What? Do you see a clue?"

"Without my phone?" Mika snickered. "No—there's food over there!"

She hurried toward the shop at the end of the block, which had a red canopy featuring a cute cartoon of a little purple creature with a big smile. Mika's stomach practically roared in response to the delicious smells wafting out. She pulled the yen from her backpack and studied the menu. Then she looked up at the man behind the counter, who smiled down at her and said something in Japanese.

Suddenly, Mika felt shy. Every single useful phrase in Japanese she'd practiced over the last few months flew out of her head. She smiled tentatively back at the server, then pointed at the menu.

"*Takoyaki?*" the server asked encouragingly. His gaze fell on Andy, who had just walked up. "*Nan mai?*"

Nan mai. Mika knew that one. "How many!" she cried triumphantly. "Two. Um. I mean, *ni.*"

"*Ni?*" The server held up two fingers, and Mika nodded, relieved. As he turned around to prepare their order, Mika grinned proudly at Andy.

"I did it! I ordered!"

"Yeah, but *what* did you order?" Andy asked.

"Ta-ko-ya-ki," Mika said slowly. "I think that's what he called it."

"Yeah, but what *is* it?"

"It's *food.*" Mika inhaled deeply. "I would eat literally anything right now."

"Even Brie?" Andy teased.

Mika pulled a face. Dad loved fancy cheeses—the smellier the cheese, the more he loved it. Mika couldn't understand it at all.

"Maybe not *anything,*" she admitted.

"I'm looking it up," Andy decided, opening a browser on his phone. "Takoyaki . . . aha! It's—"

The server reappeared holding out two paper trays, each containing eight grilled balls covered in both white and brown sauce. Mika accepted hers eagerly, and Andy took the other.

"Arigato," he said, glancing at Mika. "Um, Mika?"

But Mika had already taken a giant bite of takoyaki.

"Hot!" she exclaimed, although it came out "Awt!"

"*Atsui*," the server said with a grin. "Hot."

Mika nodded emphatically. "Aw-ee-gaw-do," she tried to say around the mouthful of food. The server laughed.

"So, any idea what you're eating?" Andy asked as they sat on the bench outside the shop.

Mika ate thoughtfully. With a light crispy texture on the outside, the ball was soft, chewy, and creamy on the inside. It was fishy and a little bit spicy thanks to the sauces. Shrugging, she popped a second one in her mouth.

"Whatever it is, I love it."

"It's octopus," Andy told her, holding out his phone.

Mika paused midchew. She glanced back at the sign hanging in front of the shop. The little purple creature beamed back at her, and she realized it had eight little tentacles. "Ah."

"Still love it?" Andy asked, grinning.

Mika had to admit, she might not have tried takoyaki if she'd known it was octopus. But she was glad she hadn't known, because it turned out octopus was delicious! Maybe Dad was right about *some* foods. She popped another one in her mouth, then pointed to Andy's tray.

"Mm-hmm. Are you going to eat yours, or can I have them?"

OLYMPIFAN UPDATE!
Special message from the Masked Medalist

Hello, OlympiFans!

I hope you're all enjoying the Games—and our game, too.
I miss the excitement of competing, but watching all of
you play my game has been a thrill! That's right,
barely one day in Tokyo, and I've already seen
OlympiFans on the streets, searching for clues.
Did any of you see me? 👀

CHAPTER FIVE
ANDY

ANDY HAD TO admit, takoyaki *was* delicious. He ate six of them, then gave in to Mika's pleading puppy-dog eyes and let her finish off his last two. After looking around for a trash can with no luck, they stuffed their paper trays, chopsticks, and napkins in Mika's backpack.

"I don't see any litter," Mika said as Andy opened *OlympiFan.* "There's got to be trash cans somewhere, or the streets wouldn't be so clean!"

Andy was already walking, eyes glued to his phone. "I'm sure we'll find one eventually. Come on, we only have half an hour to circle the block!"

Playing in AR was cooler than Andy had expected—even better than VR mode, since they were actually in the city. Through his screen, Andy saw the street ahead of him bustling with people—spotting the little animations was difficult thanks to the crowd. There were the footprints at the bottom of the screen (that still hadn't changed from blue to yellow). But when he focused on a particular spot, one of those "fun fact" bubbles would pop up, containing a piece of trivia. Andy kept swiveling his phone this way and that to read them, and he made a mental note to show Dad this feature.

Did you know Shinjuku has the busiest train station in the world?

This bakery is famous for its tasty cream puffs.

Kaiju alert—heads up for Godzilla!

Andy stopped, staring at that last animation. Then he tilted his head back and let out a surprised laugh. "Mika, look!"

His sister followed his gaze. "What? I don't—oh!"

Just around the corner, the massive head of Godzilla loomed over the roof of a hotel. Its mouth was open, sharp teeth exposed as it glared down at the street below.

"That is *awesome*," Mika said fervently. "Hang on, I've gotta take a picture . . ."

Andy waited as Mika snapped a few photos. He lifted his phone and framed Godzilla in the screen to see if *OlympiFan* had anything else to say about the monster— then his eyes went to the bottom of the screen.

His footprints were yellow.

"We're close to a clue!" Andy yelped, and Mika swiveled around to look at him.

"What? Really?"

"Yeah, come on!" He took off down the sidewalk, dodging pedestrians and keeping his eyes on the footprints. The closer he got to the hotel with the Godzilla, the more vivid the yellow footprints became. The moment he reached the entrance, the footprints began to change colors.

"They're turning pink!" Mika cried, and Andy saw she had her app open, too. The siblings dashed into the lobby, sweeping their phones around frantically to try to spot the clue. Andy forced himself to slow down, taking in the polished wood floors, the stylish sitting areas with elegant bookshelves, the concierge desk, and the statue of Godzilla lumbering past a few knee-high skyscrapers.

"Look! I bet it's over there." Andy hurried over to the roped-off statue. He stopped in front of it and framed Godzilla in his screen. His heart leapt when he saw a tiny animated note fluttering over the monster's head. Andy tapped it, and the note zoomed toward him, opening to reveal a dark green square. A second later, Team MADR's clue collection page opened, and the square joined the others. Andy watched, pleased, as the colors shuffled around again.

"Yesss!" Mika cheered. "Can I take your picture in

front of Godzilla? We should document our first clue in Tokyo!"

Andy obliged, kneeling down and pretending to cower at Godzilla's feet while Mika giggled and snapped the shot.

After leaving the hotel, Andy and Mika headed around the block, circling back to the restaurant where they were meeting Dad. This street had even bigger ads and banners looming overhead. Most of these were digital, Andy noticed, which looked really cool but made it even harder to spot the animations when they popped up on his screen. Something new caught his eye: a tiny question mark, moving down the street toward him. As it passed, Andy tapped on it, and a message appeared.

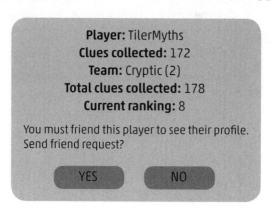

Player: TilerMyths
Clues collected: 172
Team: Cryptic (2)
Total clues collected: 178
Current ranking: 8

You must friend this player to see their profile. Send friend request?

YES   NO

Andy stopped walking. "Mika, look at this," he said, showing her his screen. "This guy's team only has two players, but somehow they've found a hundred and seventy-eight clues!"

"Hmm, wow." Mika sounded distracted.

"TilerMyths . . . I've seen that name before. I think this guy plays *S-Cape*, too! He's collected most of the clues by himself, his teammate must not . . ."

Andy stopped, because Mika was gazing up at the digital billboard directly across the street. He looked to see a giant image of a family watching the opening ceremony on television, just like the Kudos had done the night before. Two women sat on a couch, one with a gap-toothed toddler on her lap. A boy a few years younger than Andy sat cross-legged on the floor at their feet, waving a Canadian flag. All four of them looked completely riveted by the ceremony. It was a pretty cool shot, Andy had to admit—whoever took it had managed to show the television in the mirror hanging behind the couch without capturing their own reflection. The Enspire logo appeared over the image, followed by an Instagram handle and *#TeamWorld*.

When the ad vanished, replaced by an image of a Paralympic swimmer with blond hair, Mika finally tore her gaze away from the billboard. She caught Andy watching her and blushed.

"What?"

Andy raised an eyebrow. "Are you okay? You looked like you were in a trance or something."

"No, I just . . . that Enspire contest is really cool, that's all."

"What contest?"

Mika looked flustered. "You know, we saw a commercial for it during the opening ceremony. They're doing this Instagram campaign where people post photos that 'capture the spirit of unity during the Olympic Games,'" she explained, wiggling her fingers like air quotes. "You just add #TeamWorld to enter the contest, and if they like your picture, they include it in their ads." Mika gestured to the billboard again. "I mean, whoever posted that just had their picture on a giant billboard in the middle of Tokyo! Isn't that so cool?"

"Yeah, I guess." Andy started walking again, and Mika kept up next to him. He couldn't help but notice that his sister sounded weirdly nervous. Why did she care so much about some sportswear company's commercials? He was about to say something more, but then yellow footprints caught his eye. "Oh hey, we're close to another clue!"

Mika seemed relieved for the change of subject. The siblings turned back onto the street where they'd started, but on the opposite end from the takoyaki shop. The footprints began to glow brighter as they passed several small manga shops, all with flashy neon signs and cardboard cutouts of anime characters in the front windows. There was a commotion up ahead, and pedestrians started moving out of the way. Andy and Mika stepped up onto the curb as the same rowdy group of teens that had almost run them over outside of the hotel came charging down the street.

"Hi, Sabine!" Mika yelled, waving both hands over her head. Sabine spotted them and waved as she and her friends flew by.

Quickly, Andy opened the rankings page and scrolled up until he found Team SuperFan. "They're in third place," he told Mika. "Two hundred and fifty clues."

His stomach flipped over as he said it. Team MADR had some work to do if they were going to find the Bronze medal first.

Mika frowned thoughtfully. "You know, it's weird that they're all sticking together. They'd find a lot more clues if they split up, like us—you and me in one location, Devon and Riley in another."

"Maybe they're not allowed to split up," Andy pointed out. "Sabine said it's a school assignment for them, involving teamwork."

Before Mika could respond, a tall man with blond hair and a matching beard jogged past, trying to catch up with Team SuperFan. A giant video camera was perched on his shoulder, and his T-shirt read DRISCOLL PRODUCTIONS.

"Hey there! Are y'all playing *OlympiFan*?" he called after the teens in a Southern accent. The group was whooping too loudly to hear him, and a moment later, they'd disappeared around the corner. "Ah well." Sighing, the man turned and spotted Andy and Mika, both with their phones in their hands. "Hi! You wouldn't happen to be *OlympiFan* players, would you?"

"Yes," Andy began, then remembered the rules: no talking to strangers, even if they seemed perfectly nice. "Sorry, we've got to go. Bye!"

The man said something else, but Andy and Mika were already hurrying down the street. Andy watched the footprints on his phone glow pink as they neared the manga shop Team SuperFan had just left. Mika had a good point: with Devon and Riley playing in VR mode in another location, Team MADR could catch up to Team SuperFan.

Besides, Andy might not need every single clue to solve the first puzzle. He just had to figure out what those squares of color meant. A fresh wave of determination filled him as he and Mika entered the shop. Being a beta tester for the Masked Medalist's new gaming company was on the line—and Andy was going to make sure Team MADR was victorious.

TEAM ALLEYOOP CHAT ROOM

Beeyanca: GODZILLAAAAAAAA

Feebee: 😄 you're so easily distracted! LOOK FOR CLUES

Beeyanca: BUT GODZILLA!!!

Shellbee: Lolol

Shellbee: Btw I downloaded Zahir Long's video from the Gallery

Feebee: The basketball player?

Shellbee: Yup! Aaaand guess whose father owns AimBot??

Feebee: What's AimBot??

Shellbee: A gaming company! Remember playing Zombiez last summer?? Maaybe Zahir decided to design a similar game with an Olympics theme . . .

Feebee: !!!!!

TEAM GHOSTCADETS CHAT ROOM

CadetRicky: It's Chiang Li, I'm telling you guys. We don't even need the hints.

CadetKara: Chiang Li isn't fluent in English!

CadetRicky: So?

CadetKara: The Masked Medalist's Instagram posts are always in English!

CadetRicky: Oh.

CadetRicky: Well, maybe he doesn't write the posts! He could've hired someone to run his Instagram!

CadetMadison: I reeeeeally think we need the hints. 🙃

TEAM SUPERFAN CHAT ROOM

SabineTheGreat: Great job today, guys! Tomorrow morning: Harajuku. We'll meet at the Hedgehog Café at 9am sharp!

AgentAngel: 👍

DragonmasterMolly: OMG CAN WE PLAY WITH THE HEDGEHOGS??

SabineTheGreat: Of course!!!

DragonmasterMolly: 😍

IronMatt: See u guys then!

AquaMaria: ☺☺☺

CaptainArmando: Yesssssss!

SuperZuki: Ok

SuperZuki: We dropped to fifth place btw

SuperZuki: I think we need a better strategy

SuperZuki: Hello?

CHAPTER SIX
MIKA

TWELVE CLUES LATER, Mika and Andy arrived back at the skyscraper where they'd left Dad. He was standing outside talking to a petite middle-aged woman with graying hair and bright red glasses, and a younger man with spiky black hair and a row of tiny black hoop earrings running up each ear. The man remained silent as Andy and Mika approached, arms crossed, fingers drumming on his elbows.

"Hey, guys!" Dad beamed when he saw them. "Come meet Ms. Suzuki and Chef Abe."

Mika blinked in surprise. Chef Abe looked way younger than she'd expected for someone who was opening his own restaurant. Ms. Suzuki gave Mika a warm smile as she shook her hand, then Andy's, but Chef Abe just stared at his shoes. His expression was almost bashful.

"Please, call me Emi," Ms. Suzuki said. "So how are you enjoying Tokyo?"

"It's amazing," Mika said excitedly. "I ate takoyaki and saw Godzilla!"

Emi laughed. "I've stayed at the Hotel Gracery Shinjuku a few times. It's marvelous."

"Plus we found a bunch of clues there," Andy added. "We were playing *OlympiFan.* It's this game that—"

"Oh, trust me, I know all about *OlympiFan.*" Emi shook her head and smiled. "My nephew is completely obsessed. It's all he's talked about for the last month!"

"Gee, I can't imagine what that's like," Dad said jokingly, and Andy rolled his eyes.

Abruptly, Chef Abe turned to Emi and spoke in rapid Japanese. His voice was soft but his tone was urgent.

Emi's smile remained in place, but Mika thought she saw a flicker of impatience in her expression. "*Mochiron,*" she said, then turned to Dad. "Chef Abe needs to get back to his kitchen. Thanks again for doing this, Tom. I know it's very last minute, and we really appreciate it."

"Thank *you,*" Dad said emphatically, patting his laptop bag. "I'm really looking forward to getting started on this profile. And I can't wait for opening night, Chef."

Chef Abe flashed a quick, almost nervous smile. "Thank you," he whispered. Then turned and hurried inside the building. Dad turned back to Emi, his expression bewildered.

"I don't think he likes me."

Emi gave him a small smile. "He does! He's just very

shy. Unless he's watching sports—you should hear him when he's watching a baseball game. He gets so worked up! Cheering one second, then yelling the next. It's really pretty funny."

"I can't imagine him yelling," Mika said. "He's so quiet!"

"I have to say, I'm curious to see him in action," Dad admitted. "He's pretty young to be managing a kitchen staff."

"He's young, but trust me, he's more than capable of calling the shots. You'll see!" Emi winked and then hurried after the chef.

Mika snorted. "Does she mean he yells at people or something?"

"That's hard to imagine," Dad said, chuckling. "It took a while for me to get him to actually talk during our interview." Clapping his hands together, he looked from Mika to Andy. "So! Are you two ready for a late dinner, or are you too full of takoyaki?"

"I'm ready!" Mika exclaimed, and her stomach rumbled in agreement.

Mika totally wanted to explore Tokyo some more after dinner with her family. But before she even finished her soba noodles, her eyelids started drooping. Across the table, Andy yawned so loudly their waiter laughed.

"Jet lag," Dad said with a grin. "You guys will sleep well tonight!"

"It's only eight thirty," Mika protested.

"Which is four thirty in LA," Mom pointed out. "In the *morning*."

Mika wanted to argue, but Andy's yawn was contagious. Before she knew it, they were back at the hotel, and Mika barely remembered crawling into her bed before falling into a deep sleep.

The next morning, Dad opened the door to Mika and Andy's room. "Rise and shine!" he said cheerfully. "Don't want to sleep through your first Olympic event!"

Mika tried to respond, but all that came out was another yawn, as Andy mumbled something incoherent into his pillow.

Dad laughed. "Jet lag is tough the first few days. Best thing to do is get up and at 'em!"

After a quick breakfast at the hotel, the three of them headed for the nearest subway station. Mika liked taking trains and buses when they visited other cities—it was so different from LA, where they went almost everywhere by car. A few stops later, they stepped out onto a platform and headed for the stairs. Mika noticed an ad for Enspire on the wall, and her stomach did a flip-flop. Andy had definitely been looking at her strangely when he'd caught her staring at that billboard. Honestly, she couldn't blame him, considering she'd been rambling uncontrollably about the contest. Did he suspect what she'd done?

As they exited the station, Andy yawned again. "Did you stay up all night playing *OlympiFan* again?" Mika teased, and he rolled his eyes.

"No, but I'm still tired."

The truth was, Mika still felt pretty sleepy, too. She stifled her own yawn as they walked to the gymnastics arena.

But the moment they entered the atrium, Mika felt a jolt and was wide awake. The place was practically crackling with energy, packed with enthusiastic fans chatting about the Games. Massive flat-screen TVs hung on the walls, all displaying the day's highlights so far: scenes from weight lifting, tennis, boxing, and swimming events surrounded Mika as she moved through the crowd.

Inside the enormous arena, Dad led them to their seats. Mika sat, then immediately stood up and pointed. "I see Mom!" she cried excitedly. Tables lined both sides of the floor, and Mom was with her two Compete staff writers at a table near the left corner, all stationed behind laptops. Wesley Brooks and Hana Takahashi were there, too.

As Mika looked over the crowd, her mind went back to the Enspire campaign. *During the Olympic Games, photos capturing the spirit of unity will be featured in our campaign to be seen throughout Tokyo and the rest of the world . . .*

Applause broke out, and Mika snapped back to attention as an American gymnast walked toward the end of the mat and faced the vault. The announcer was speaking, but Mika barely heard him; her heart was suddenly hammering extra hard against her chest. She couldn't believe she was about to watch an actual Olympic athlete, and Mika was equal parts thrilled to be a spectator and nervous for this girl who'd been working so hard for years to prepare for this moment.

Captivated, the crowd watched as the gymnast raised her arms and smiled confidently. Suddenly, with a look of fierce concentration, she lowered her arms, and Mika held her breath as the gymnast lunged forward, sprinting toward the vault. Then she was in the air, flipping onto the vault in a handstand and springing up higher than ever, executing a series of what seemed to Mika like a dozen twists in a split second before landing on her feet, spreading her arms wide in triumph.

The crowd burst into cheers, and Mika let out her breath in a *whoosh.*

"*Wow!*" exclaimed Andy enthusiastically. Mika nodded, but she couldn't even speak. She remembered watching the Olympics on TV in the past, but seeing an Olympic event in person was different. Her pulse was still pounding in her ears as the gymnast waited for her score.

Mika thought of the picture she and Andy had seen earlier, the one with the two moms and their kids watching the opening ceremony. She could clearly see why Enspire had chosen it as part of their campaign. The photographer had perfectly captured the looks of wonder on all of their faces. What if Mika could capture this feeling she was experiencing right now in the arena?

She scanned the crowd around her again and noticed two little girls sitting side by side. One had shiny black pigtails and a shirt with a purple unicorn on the front. On her other side was a man Mika assumed was the girl's father, and both were waving red flags with yellow stars—China, Mika was pretty sure. The second little girl had short, wavy brown hair and tons of freckles covering her nose and cheeks. She sat next to an equally freckly teenager—her sister, Mika guessed—whose sleeve she was tugging on insistently.

Mika watched as the little girl whispered in her sister's ear. The older girl smiled, then dug around in her purse and pulled out a miniature flag with two vertical red stripes and a maple leaf in the middle, which the little girl took eagerly.

"Thanks!" she exclaimed, her voice high and bubbly, waving the Canadian flag.

Andy elbowed Mika in the side, and she swiveled around, feeling guilty for no reason. "What?"

"You're going to miss it!"

Mika looked down at the floor just as the second gymnast sprinted across the mat. The crowd gasped as she launched off the vault and performed a complicated twist—then groaned when she landed and stumbled forward a few steps before raising her arms. Even with the mistake, the applause was still deafening, and Mika cheered with everyone else as the gymnast walked toward her coach. Turning, Mika looked at the two little girls again.

They were examining one another's flags, both babbling away. Neither girl seemed to mind that they couldn't understand each other.

Casting a quick glance at Dad and Andy, Mika pulled out her phone and opened the camera. She held it at her side and watched as the next gymnast, this one from Brazil, took her place.

The gymnast raised her arms. When she began sprinting across the mat, Mika turned away and framed the two little girls in her screen. Both were waving their flags frantically as they stared intently at the gymnast. The Canadian girl grabbed the Chinese girl's hand, and Mika heard the gymnast's palms hit the vault.

The hairs on the back of Mika's neck stood up during the brief moment that followed as the gymnast flipped through the air. Time seemed to slow as Mika took the photo—then there was a light *thump* as the gymnast landed and the crowd went wild.

Dad and Andy were both cheering, and Mika whirled around to face forward before either of them noticed she'd been turned away for the whole thing. "That was so cool!" Andy said, grinning at her.

Mika nodded enthusiastically but didn't respond. Although she was dying to check out her photo, she didn't want Dad and Andy to know she'd taken it. Not that there was anything bad about taking a picture. Mika hadn't done anything *wrong*.

Yet.

After the Brazilian gymnast's scores were announced, the music returned to full volume and the level of chatter rose as everyone discussed the rankings so far. Mika sat back in her chair and, after a quick glance at Dad and Andy, opened the photo. She stifled a gasp.

It was *perfect*. Both girls were sharply in focus, their eyes shining, their mouths open in expressions of pure amazement. Their fingers were laced together tightly, each girl clutching her country's flag in her free hand. Quickly, Mika opened her photo-editing app and made a few small adjustments, bringing out the stadium lights reflected in the girls' eyes and brightening the colors on their flags. Then, glancing nervously at Dad and Andy, she opened Instagram and pulled up the edited photo.

"Oh boy. That's a fantastic photo!"

Mika jumped at the sound of the voice behind her, nearly dropping her phone. She and Andy turned to look at the man sitting behind them. He gave them a friendly smile.

"Sorry, didn't mean to snoop," he said in a Southern accent. "But that's professional quality, in my opinion."

"Thanks," Mika said, flattered. Then she noticed his T-shirt: DRISCOLL PRODUCTIONS. "Oh, we saw you in Shinjuku!" she exclaimed. "You had that giant camera, right?"

"That sounds like me," the man responded cheerfully. "I'm—"

"Gavin?" Dad leaned back in his seat to better see the man. "Gavin Driscoll, right?"

The man's face lit up. "Tom Kudo! Oh man, I can't believe I didn't recognize you sooner!"

Both men half stood in their seats to shake hands, then settled back down. "We met back when I took that trip to Argentina a few years ago," Dad explained to Andy and Mika. "Gavin makes travel documentaries. Gavin, these are my kids, Andy and Mika."

"Great to meet you both!" Gavin said, beaming at them. "Tom, I was just telling your daughter she could be a professional photographer. Did you see this shot she just got?"

Mika's face burned. A strange mix of guilt and pride flooded through her as she quickly switched back to her camera roll and held out her phone for Dad and Andy to see the photo. Dad let out a whistle.

"Mika, that's really impressive!"

"Did you take it during the Brazilian gymnast's turn?" Andy asked, and Mika nodded.

"I saw these girls before she came out," she explained. "And I thought . . . they were cute."

She wasn't sure how to explain the real reason she'd taken their picture. She'd been struck with a sudden desire to capture the anticipation and thrill on the girls' faces as they watched an amazing athlete do what she did best.

"You've got a photographer's eye," Gavin told her, and Mika flushed again from the praise.

"Thank you," she said, pocketing her phone.

"So, Gavin, I'm guessing you're here covering the Games?" Dad asked.

"You bet," Gavin said, pulling out a package of gum and unwrapping a piece. "I'm working on two documentaries. One's about the impact the Olympic and Paralympic Games have on tourism in host cities."

"Nice! I wish we could stay in Tokyo for the Paralympics," Dad said. "They're so inspiring! My wife, Karen, will be covering them, but the kids and I will have to watch from home. What's the other documentary about?"

"This new game that's apparently all the rage right now. *OlympiFan?*"

"Oh, awesome!" Mika blurted out, at the same time as Andy exclaimed, "We're playing *OlympiFan!*"

Dad shot Gavin a rueful grin. "You've opened the floodgates now, I'm afraid. These guys haven't stopped talking about that game all summer."

"Really?" Gavin looked delighted. "Well, maybe I should interview you two sometime! With your dad's permission, of course."

"Yeah, cool! That'd be awesome!" Andy said eagerly. "Do you have any idea who the Masked Medalist is?"

"I've heard a few names, but it's all just speculation," Gavin said. "Chiang Li's come up more than once. He's a table tennis champ and he's got a bunch of degrees in software development and programming. I saw him out in the lobby, actually, so I guess he's in here somewhere . . ."

He trailed off as the crowd fell silent again, and all four of them looked down at the floor, where another gymnast was taking her place on the mat. "Well, we can chat about that later." Gavin winked, then leaned back in his seat.

Mika watched as the gymnast prepared for her turn. She was still glowing from Gavin's praise. A professional filmmaker thought she was a good photographer! And Dad and Andy had been really impressed by her picture of the two little girls, too.

Maybe Mika actually did have a talent for photography. Didn't she deserve the chance to show it off?

After the gymnastics event was over for the day, Dad led Andy and Mika outside. The afternoon sky was a blazing blue. "Are you guys up for a little walk?" Dad asked.

"Sure!" Andy already had his phone out. "Bet I can find a few more clues. No one's gotten the Bronze medal yet!"

Sighing, Dad shook his head. "You're not going to have your eyes glued to the screen the whole time, are you? We're here to explore Tokyo!"

"But *OlympiFan* is great for exploring Tokyo," Andy told him eagerly. "Watch."

Mika trailed behind them as Andy showed Dad how little facts popped up about the locations they passed. She thought about her photo, and about Gavin's praise, and her fingers grazed her pocket. Before she could take out her phone, Dad turned around and held out his arm. A moment later, a taxi pulled over and the doors clicked open.

"I thought we were going for a walk?" Andy asked, confused.

Dad smiled. "Just wait."

A short cab ride later, Mika and Andy climbed out of the cab and stood on a boardwalk. After Dad finished paying, he joined them.

"I thought you might like to walk across Tokyo Bay!"

He pointed, and Mika and Andy turned to look at the enormous white bridge that crossed the water. On the other side, Mika could see the Tokyo skyline.

"That view is amazing!" she said excitedly.

Dad looked pleased at her reaction. "This is the Rainbow Bridge. It has solar-powered lights that get energy from the sun all day, then come on at night in all different colors!"

"Ooh, we'll have to come back at night to see it!" Mika already had her phone out, and she took a few pictures, balancing on her toes to get the best angle.

She kept her phone out as they started walking, and soon Dad and Andy were back in conversation about *OlympiFan*. Mika gazed at the bridge, but her thoughts were back on the gymnasts. She pictured their determined expressions, the way they had launched themselves full speed at the vault without hesitation or fear. And then she made a decision.

Mika swiped to the last page on her phone, where just one app icon waited. She'd downloaded Instagram after seeing that Enspire commercial during the opening ceremony, and with Riley sending her encouraging texts, she'd set up an anonymous account: bluedreamphotos. She'd never broken a rule this big before. Sure, she'd slipped table scraps to Lily and Po during meals, but this was different.

A photography contest was a big deal, and Mika felt she deserved a chance to share her photos. Fingers trembling slightly, Mika pulled up her edited photo of the two little girls. She added #TeamWorld to the caption, then tapped share on the top right of the screen. Moments later, her photo appeared in her feed. A wave of giddiness passed over her as she closed the app and stuffed her phone back in her pocket.

Done, she thought, pulse racing. And there would be plenty of opportunities for more photos while she was in Tokyo. After their trip, Mika would delete the account so her parents would never have to know. With a little luck, millions of people might see one of her photos.

Mika felt a little thrill at the thought, and she smiled to herself as she hurried to catch up with Dad and Andy.

TilerMyths
Team: Cryptic

AndyK has sent you a friend
request. Accept?

 YES NO

CHAPTER SEVEN
ANDY

THE WEEK FELT like it was flying by. Andy was having a blast: he and Mika spent hours exploring the area surrounding their hotel while Dad wrote, and in the evenings they got to attend the Olympic Games with Mom and her staff. Andy and Mika had visited an origami museum, tried more food (karaage was just as tasty as Dad had promised), bought manga books and figurines for Devon and Riley, and watched archery, diving, and taekwondo.

Somehow during all of that, Andy's team had managed to collect two hundred and three clues! Their total was now over three hundred, but Andy still hadn't figured out what the color squares actually meant. He checked the *OlympiFan* scoreboard several times an hour, and he and Mika had both friended lots of players. Several teams had fizzled out after the first few days, probably because there was so much to see and do at the Olympics. Now Team MADR was hovering around fifteenth place. Team SuperFan stayed in the top ten. And Team Cryptic had been in first place for almost the entire day—thanks mostly to TilerMyths, who'd some-how collected almost four hundred clues by himself (and finally accepted Andy's friend request).

Even with all those clues, TilerMyths obviously hadn't figured out what the color squares meant, because Team Cryptic hadn't found the Bronze medal yet. Andy didn't care if he didn't have as many clues; he was going to fig-ure out where that medal was first.

He studied the squares over breakfast Thursday morn-ing. The hotel's buffet was huge, and included all the breakfast foods Andy and Mika loved, like scrambled eggs and French toast. But there were lots of other choices too: miso soup, grilled fish, rice, tofu, and *tamagoyaki,* a sweetened omelet that Andy really liked.

French toast was Mika's favorite, but she'd decided to try one new thing every morning along with it. She placed her tray down across from Andy, and he peered curiously at the small bowl of white rice topped with what looked like slimy beans.

"What's that?"

"*Natto,*" Mika announced. "I looked it up—fermented soybeans." She pulled apart her chopsticks and scooped up a little bite, her brows immediately knitting together.

"Don't like it?"

Mika swallowed, then took a sip of milk. "It's . . . interesting. It's an *acquired taste.*"

Andy laughed. "*Acquired taste* is exactly what Dad said about Brie, and you haven't acquired *that* yet."

"Okay, but this is way better than Brie." Mika pretended to shudder. "Old socks probably taste better than Brie." She ate several more bites of natto before putting the chopsticks down. A message notification popped up in the Team MADR chat room, and Andy tapped it while Mika began drowning her French toast in maple syrup.

> **Devon:** RED ALERT! The MM posted on Instagram . . . weren't you guys there??

A link was included under Devon's message. Andy opened it, stopping with a bite of tamagoyaki halfway to his mouth when an Instagram post filled his screen. "Mika! The Masked Medalist posted!"

"Ooh!" Mika leaned across the table, and Andy showed her the photo of a gymnast, arms raised in victory after her landing. "Wait . . . That *is* the same event we saw!" Mika said excitedly. "That's the gymnast from Team USA!"

"The Masked Medalist was *there*." Andy couldn't believe they'd been so close to the mysterious creator of *OlympiFan*. Then he remembered something. "Hang on—what was the name of the table tennis player Gavin told us about, the one a bunch of players think is the Masked Medalist . . . Something Li?"

"Chiang Li!" Mika said immediately. "And Gavin said he *saw* him there!"

The siblings exchanged a grin. "I guess Chiang Li's

at the top of our list so far," Andy said excitedly. He scrolled down so he and Mika could read the post below the picture.

> I have been enjoying the Games, and I hope you OlympiFans are enjoying our game just as much! Although an impressive number of clues have been found, the Bronze is still hidden. If you want to win, you'd better start looking at the big picture!

"Big picture," Andy said, his heart pounding in his ears. "Maybe . . . maybe that's a hint."

He opened *OlympiFan* again as Mika pulled out her own phone. Andy stared at his team's collection of clues. He'd already noticed that when new color squares were added and they all reshuffled, similar colors would land close to each other: a dark blue square would move near the other blues, while the only pink square would zoom over to the reds. Most of the squares were some shade of green, brown, or blue, along with a lot of black, gray, and a pearly sort of white. He'd tried zooming out, so that more of the squares filled the page. When they'd realign again, just a little, he couldn't figure out why. Very few squares were the exact same color; the shades were always a little different.

While Mika replied to Devon's message, Andy zoomed out and watched the squares shimmy around. He zoomed out more and more as the squares grew tinier and tinier until they started to blur together. Kind of like . . .

"Pixels!" Andy cried, and Mika jumped. "They're pixels—this is a photo!"

"Seriously?" Mika stared when he showed her his screen. "Okay, but we're still missing a lot of clues. If you're right, it'd take us forever to get every single pixel in that picture."

"We don't need every single one." Andy was already back in their team chat room, typing a message to Devon and Riley.

Andy: The squares are pixels, and the photo is a picture of where the Bronze is hidden. Zoom out and see if you recognize anything!

Quickly, he opened the clues again. This time, he zoomed out as far as he could go. Mika was right: so far, their photo had more white space than pixels. But most of the black and dark gray pixels were on the left, and the pearly white ones were on the right. The greens, browns, and blues seemed to be part of the background, while the black and white shapes were in the forefront. Andy thought something about it looked familiar. He blinked, and a moment later, it hit him.

"It looks like a wedding photo." He placed his phone flat on the table and turned it to face Mika. "Look— think about that photo in our living room, the one of Grandma and Grandpa on their wedding day. It was outdoors, there were trees behind them, right? And they're both wearing kimonos." Andy jabbed the picture twice. "Black for Grandpa, white for Grandma."

"*Oh.*" Mika's eyes widened. "Oh my god, I think you're right! Except . . ." She paused, chewing her lip. "The Bronze medal can't be at an actual wedding."

"Right." Andy felt momentarily defeated. Then he opened the chat room again and messaged Devon and Riley.

> **Andy:** It's a wedding photo! Where do people like to get married in Tokyo?

Mika read the message and frowned. "There's probably a gazillion popular places for weddings," she groaned. "There's got to be a bigger clue in this photo."

Andy was already doing a Google search. His stomach plummeted when he saw how many results came up. Hotels, chapels, shrines . . . He thought of the trees, and added *outdoors* to his search, but it didn't really help.

"The brown pixels," Mika was saying slowly. "The ones on the left look like part of a tree trunk. But the ones on the right are horizontal, and kind of curve up."

Andy glanced at her screen, then did a double take. He'd just been scrolling through pictures of buildings with that exact same shape in their design! "It's a shrine or a temple or something!" he exclaimed, thumbs flying over his screen. "I bet that's it—see? Shrines all have gates just like that! Now we just have to figure out *which* shrine."

They both returned to their phones to find Riley adding rapid-fire messages in the forum.

> **Riley:** Meiji Jingu, maybe???

> **Riley:** It's a shrine. I remember reading that it's really popular for weddings.

> **Riley:** Ugh I just tried going there in VR mode, the line's already long.

> **Devon:** 15 minute wait! 😔

Andy groaned. To try to keep things as fair as possible between VR and AR players, *OlympiFan* made VR players wait in line based on the distance from their last destination. After all, AR players couldn't just magically pop up in a destination halfway across the city. Although right now, Andy wished desperately that he could. No two teams had the exact same collection of clues, which meant they all had different parts of the photo. If this many VR players were trying to get into the Meiji Shrine, then Team MADR wasn't the only team to suspect this was where the Bronze medal was hidden.

"Andy." Mika looked up from her phone, her eyes wide with excitement. "That shrine is really close to the stadium where we watched the handball event. It's only three subway stops away!"

Andy sat up straighter. "Really? Let's—wait, we can't go. Dad's working until lunch."

"So let's ask him if we can take the train by ourselves!" Mika was already standing and picking up her tray. "The rule was no public transportation *unless* it's a route we've done with him or Mom already, right?"

Half a minute later, Andy and Mika burst into the business room across the lobby from the breakfast area. Dad looked up from his laptop, startled.

"You guys okay?" he asked, and Andy and Mika explained everything as fast as they could. Dad leaned back in his chair, frowning. "You think you remember how to get there?"

"Yamanote Line, three stops, get off at Harajuku Station," Mika recited immediately, and Andy gave her a grateful look. Knowing Mika, she'd probably taken notes on the route the day before.

"Still have your metro cards?"

"Yes!"

Dad nodded. "Okay, let's go over the rest of the rules one more time."

"No talking to strangers, and no splitting up," Andy said quickly.

Mika patted her little blue backpack. "Always have yen on us."

"Basically, no doing anything dumb," Andy finished. "Can we go now? *Please?*"

"All right." Dad glanced at the clock on the wall. "Text me when you get there and keep me updated. Be back here in time for lunch, okay?"

"Thanks, Dad!" Andy was already sprinting from the room, Mika on his heels.

The train ride was short, but Andy couldn't stop checking the *OlympiFan* app. The first few players were about to enter the shrine—and of course, TilerMyths was one of them.

Devon: Are you guys going?

ANDY: YES!

Devon: YESSSS!!!

Riley: Awesome! I just added a bunch of clues and I think the couple in the photo is standing in front of the torii.

Andy: What's that?

Riley: The gate! I looked it up, and it's HUGE— you can't miss it. I bet the medal is there!

Andy: Thx!

Andy's palms began to sweat as the train slowed to a stop at Harajuku Station. The moment the doors slid open, he and Mika rushed toward the stairs. Above ground, they stopped on the street, panting, and looked around.

"There!" Mika pointed to a sign. Below the Japanese letters, it read MEIJI JINGU, and beneath that was an arrow.

Andy and Mika took off again, and a few seconds later they were crossing a stone bridge. Massively tall trees lined either side of the wide path, which was crowded with people strolling leisurely in and out of the park.

"Whoa!" Mika gasped as the *torii* came into view. Riley was right, Andy thought—the gate was *huge,* a beautiful wooden structure with two pillars supporting crosspieces that towered almost as high as the surrounding trees.

Andy slowed to a quick walk, opening AR mode in the *OlympiFan* app. The footprints glowed yellow . . . no, not yellow. *Bronze.* Andy let out an excited yelp.

"Riley was right! The medal's somewhere around the gate!"

Before he could take another step, Mika grabbed his arm. "Do you hear that?"

Andy was about to ask what she meant when he heard it: the unmistakable whoops and shouts of Team SuperFan. Turning around, Andy saw the group of teens sprinting across the bridge.

"Hurry!" he yelled, and he and Mika rushed toward the gate. Andy watched the bronze footprints turn yellow again once he had passed under the crossbeams and stood on the other side. Gasping for breath, Andy whirled around and stared through his screen. He could see SabineTheGreat's avatar among the others as Team

SuperFan drew closer. But where was the medal? Andy doubled back and stopped directly under the gate, turning full circle and trying to spot it around all of the people passing in and out of the park. His footprints stayed bronze, but he couldn't see it anywhere. Nearby, Mika was doing the same thing. Team SuperFan was only a few yards away—and they looked ready to plow right over Andy and Mika.

Suddenly, Andy had an idea. Tilting his head back, he held up his phone and stared through its screen at the horizontal beam high overhead. His heart leapt when he caught a flicker of something, and he zoomed in with shaky fingers.

A Bronze medal hung from the lower beam of the gate.

Andy blinked, stunned. As determined as he'd been to find one of the medals, part of him hadn't actually expected to win. He started to tap the screen to claim the medal, but a passing tourist jostled him and he nearly dropped his phone. Quickly, Andy zoomed back in on the spot.

The medal was gone.

Andy's confusion only lasted a moment. Because then his screen changed to an explosion of confetti. A message appeared, and Andy's heart plummeted.

OLYMPIFAN UPDATE!
Bronze Medal Found!

Found by TilerMyths (VR)

**Congratulations to the Bronze Medalists:
TEAM CRYPTIC!!!**

CHAPTER EIGHT
MIKA

"YOU'VE GOT TO be *kidding* me!"

Mika gaped at the message on her screen. She looked up, half expecting to see Team Cryptic nearby celebrating even though she knew TilerMyths had won in VR mode. Instead, she saw Team SuperFan come to a halt a few feet away as they saw the notification, too.

"Ugggh," one girl groaned, pulling the giant Mexican flag hat off her head. The others looked as disappointed as she was; one of them, a tall guy in oversize sunglasses, stalked away from the group, as if the loss had been his fault. Sabine called after him, but he ignored her, his expression angry and dejected.

For a moment, Mika actually felt bad for them until she realized how close she and Andy had come to winning. Two teenage girls jogged up to the gate, slowing down and looking at their phones. One glanced up and saw Mika watching her.

"Hey! Are you on Team Cryptic?"

"Nope!" Mika replied, noticing that the girls both wore yellow-and-black-striped knee socks and matching necklaces with bee pendants. "Team MADR."

"Oh, you're MikaK!" The girl smiled. "We friended each other a few days ago. I'm Phoebe, and this is Bianca. Team ALLEYOOP."

"Hi!" Mika smiled back. "I like your socks."

"Thanks!"

"Team Cryptic is playing in VR mode," Bianca pointed out, gesturing to Phoebe's screen. "They're not here."

"Ah, right." Phoebe sighed. "I can't believe the medal was right here just a few seconds ago!"

"Come on, Shelby's probably wondering where we are . . ."

The girls headed slowly toward the bridge, and Andy turned to Mika. He looked dazed. "I saw it," he said as they moved to the side of the path. He gestured up at the gate. "I saw the Bronze medal in my screen. I almost had it . . ."

Mika patted his arm. "Well, it's really cool that we came so close," she pointed out kindly. "And there are still two medals left!"

"That's true." Andy sighed. "The clues to the Silver will be released in an hour, so we can start searching again. I bet TilerMyths is already looking since his team got those new locations as soon as they found the Bronze—a head start was part of the prize, right? Oh, I wonder if they decided to go for one hint and five hundred points, or two hints and two hundred fifty points . . ."

He began scrolling through the app again. After waiting to make sure he was distracted, Mika turned her attention to her own phone. The last time she'd checked her photo of the two little girls at the gymnastics event had been right before bed the previous night, and she had forty comments. She'd been dying to check on it again all morning, but she was too nervous that Andy or Dad might see. Now, Mika turned to face Andy and opened Instagram. When she saw the number of notifications on her photo, she gasped.

Andy glanced up. "What?"

"Nothing! Just a text from Riley," Mika replied, trying to keep her voice light. Andy went back to his phone, and Mika stared down at her notifications again.

One hundred and fifty-four likes. Seventy-six comments. And forty-two new followers.

Mika scrolled through the latest comments, exhaling shakily. As she read, she felt an uncontrollable grin stretch across her cheeks.

BEAUTIFUL!!!

Omg look at these little girls! This is perfection!

Wow! Followed—I hope you post more pics like this!

Hey @enspire, this is the best #TeamWorld pic yet!!!

Love it!

Sooo cute!!!

A thought occurred to Mika, and she checked to see who had liked her photo. One of the first accounts had been rileyreallyreads, which had made her giggle when she'd seen it a few days earlier. Riley had promised not to follow her right away, because they'd both agreed that would probably make it too obvious that it was Mika's secret account. But Riley hadn't been able to resist liking the post immediately. Mika scrolled through the rest of the names, amazed that so many people had seen her photo. Then she saw the last account and pressed her lips together hard to keep from squealing.

The official Enspire account had commented with a thumbs-up emoji!

Mika fought the urge to do a happy dance right there in the park. Of course, whoever ran Enspire's Instagram account was probably liking all of the posts under *#TeamWorld*. But the point was they'd seen it. Maybe they'd actually choose it for their campaign! Mika was so absorbed in her phone that she didn't notice someone standing next to her until they spoke.

"Are you guys playing that *OlympiFan* game?"

Mika almost jumped out of her skin. The person, a round-faced girl about her age with brown skin and a cloud of black curls, held up her hands and laughed.

"Sorry! I didn't mean to scare you." She had a gentle accent and a friendly grin.

"It's okay," Mika said, returning the smile. "Yeah, we were playing *OlympiFan*—my brother actually almost got the Bronze!"

"It was *so close*," Andy said with an exaggerated sigh.

"Aw, I'm sorry!" the girl exclaimed. "I just saw the notification that someone found it, but I can't believe it was *here*. My mom and I were right across the street buying souvenirs for my grandparents. I'm Emma, by the way."

"I'm Mika, and this is my brother, Andy," Mika said. "So you're playing, too?"

"Yeah, but I'm not very good." Emma shrugged. "I really like all the facts that pop up when you use AR mode, though. Do you guys live here?"

"No, we're from Los Angeles," Andy told her. "What about you?"

"Johannesburg." A note of pride crept into Emma's voice, and she pointed to the pins on the strap of her purse: a South African flag, a silhouette of someone sprinting, and the Olympic logo. "My brother's competing in the Olympics. He's a hurdler."

"Oh my god, that's so cool!" Mika exclaimed. "We're here for the Olympics, too. Our mom's here for work. She's the editor of Compete—a sports website," she added. "When's your brother's event? Maybe we can go watch!"

"It's Sunday! The hundred-and-ten-meter hurdle." Emma glanced up at the gate and gave Mika a sheepish look. "Hey, would you mind taking a picture of me standing under the gate? I tried to get a selfie, but it's too tall."

"Sure!" Mika took Emma's phone, then hurried to stand several yards away from the gate. Emma stood directly beneath it, arms spread wide and beaming like a gymnast who'd just stuck her landing. Laughing, Mika snapped the picture.

"Thanks!" Emma called, jogging over to her and taking back her phone. "I should get back to the shop. I just wanted to see where the Bronze medal had been found."

Mika was about to say goodbye when something occurred to her. "Hey, if you have any free time, maybe you can come look for clues with me and Andy sometime!"

Emma blinked. "Oh! Umm . . . sure, thanks! But I'm really not very good at that game. And your brother seems . . ." She paused, glancing over to where Andy still stood in the same spot, staring intently at his phone. "Really serious about it."

Mika snickered. "Yeah, he loves games. He takes all of them really seriously. But it doesn't matter, I promise. It'd be fun to play together!"

"Okay, yeah!" Emma pulled out her phone. "What's your number?"

Mika recited her phone number as Emma typed. A moment later, a text popped up on Mika's phone:

Hi! It's Emma Botha.

"Got it!" Mika said.

A soft twinkling melody sounded, and Emma glanced at the screen. "Ah, that's my mom. I gotta go! Maybe we can meet up later this week?"

"That'd be great!" Mika replied.

With a cheerful wave, Emma headed back to the bridge. Turning to look up at the beautiful, massive gate again, Mika thought of Emma's photo. Mika had been so preoccupied with the Enspire campaign, she hadn't taken many pictures in Tokyo that included herself.

"Andy!" she called, and he looked up. "Take my picture!"

"Okay!"

Mika jogged over to the spot where Emma had stood directly beneath the gate. She could see Emma crossing the bridge, not far behind Phoebe and Bianca and their eye-catching socks.

A familiar laugh caught her attention. She glanced around and spotted Gavin Driscoll, giant camera up on his shoulder, chatting with the SuperFan player wearing the oversize sunglasses. Gavin was chuckling as they spoke, but the boy still looked upset as he gestured at his teammates, who stood farther down the path. Mika

could see Sabine watching the boy and rolling her eyes. Apparently, the "fostering team-building" part of their school assignment wasn't going so well.

"Ready!" Andy called.

Turning, Mika grinned and raised her arms as if reaching to touch the gate's beam. After Andy took the picture, Mika took a step toward him—then stopped.

A small square of paper lay on the ground, right where she'd been standing. Mika saw something scrawled on it in bright purple ink. She read the message, blinked in disbelief, then read it again.

Congratulations! You found the REAL clue. Pandas stand guard around the Silver.

TEAM DRAGONFLAME CHAT ROOM

GoblinGeorge: I was in the VR line RIGHT BEHIND TilerMyths! 😞

CentaurCici: ARGH!!!

MageMisaki: Sorry it took me so long to get there! But I looked around the gate for a while after Team Cryptic won, and you guys aren't going to believe what I found.

CentaurCici: ??

MageMisaki: I'll show you when we meet up at the hotel.

TEAM ALLEYOOP CHAT ROOM

Shellbee: Why are you guys still at the park??

Feebee: Leaving now, sorry! B had an EPIC idea.

Shellbee: ??

Beeyanca: 😎

TEAM CRYPTIC CHAT ROOM

UppeRcase: Mission accomplished!

TilerMyths: 👍

CHAPTER NINE
ANDY

"ANDY!"

A couple strolling under the gate cast curious glances at Mika, who was crouched on the ground, waving frantically. Frowning, Andy hurried over to join his sister.

"What is it?" He saw the paper on the ground, and squatted to get a better look. When he read the message, his stomach flipped over.

"Is it . . . I mean, do you think . . ." Mika's voice was hushed. "Did the Masked Medalist actually leave this here?"

Andy's mind was reeling. "Maybe? I mean, *OlympiFan* could have another level—a secret level, like the time travel portal in *S-Cape,* or the—"

"But what about the VR players? This isn't fair to them."

"Oh." Andy had to admit it was a good point. *Olympi-Fan* had obviously been designed to be as fair as possible to both AR and VR players.

"Plus, it's in English," Mika added.

"Well, the Masked Medalist's Instagram posts are all in English," Andy pointed out. "That doesn't mean English is their first language. But you're right—this note doesn't seem like an official clue. It's not a puzzle, like the color squares. It's just telling us where to find the medal."

"Hmm." Mika bit her lip. "Should we take it?"

Andy barely heard her. He was still trying to think through what had just happened. "I looked on the ground for the medal . . ." he said slowly, remembering. "Through my phone. I looked on the ground, then to both sides, and then I looked up and saw it. I would've noticed this note."

"So you think whoever put it here did it *after* Tiler-Myths won?" Mika looked doubtful. "That was only like ten minutes ago!"

The Kudo kids looked at each other, then shot to their feet, staring around wildly. Team SuperFan was still talking to Gavin Driscoll. There were probably other *OlympiFan* players here among the tourists. Had Andy and Mika been looking at their phones while one of them left the note on the ground?

Of course, there was another possibility, too. Andy couldn't help imagining the Masked Medalist hiding behind a tree, watching them. What if they'd come here to see the action?

Kneeling, Andy picked up the clue. "There's something on the back!" Mika exclaimed, and he turned it over to see tiny black lettering printed on the bottom of the note.

コンチネンタルホテル赤坂
CONTINENTAL HOTEL AKASAKA

"Whoa." Mika stared at Andy, eyes wide. "So whoever left this is probably staying at this hotel?"

Andy nodded, his spirits lifting again.

Now *this* was a clue. Not a clue to the location of the Silver medal, but a clue to the identity of whoever had left this note—and maybe even to the Masked Medalist's identity.

"I look *so* professional." Mika adjusted the day pass hanging around her neck and beamed. "Thanks for getting us these passes, Mom!"

Mom smiled as she handed Andy his day pass, which was attached to a blue lanyard. The pass read GUEST, COMPETE MEDIA. Andy hung it around his neck, lost in thought until Mom cleared her throat.

Andy jumped. "What?"

"You're so out of it!" Mom said, looking amused. "I thought you'd be more excited about this."

"I am!" Andy stepped off the escalator and followed Mom and Mika, feeling slightly guilty. The Continental Hotel Akasaka wasn't close to where the Kudos were staying, and he'd spent the subway ride back trying to come up with a good reason to convince Dad to take them there. But Mom had been waiting for them with a surprise—she was taking them to the International Broadcast Center.

Still, Andy couldn't stop thinking about that note— and more importantly, whoever had written it. Even though he knew the note couldn't actually be a part of *OlympiFan*, Andy couldn't help wondering . . . what if it *was*? What if Team MADR had a clue that no other team knew about?

What if they could win the Silver? Then they'd have two hints to the Masked Medalist's identity—three, if the Medalist was staying at the Continental Hotel Akasaka.

"All right." Mom came to a halt outside a set of double doors. Her eyes were shining with anticipation. "I know I promised you guys lunch, and we'll head to the cafeteria soon, I swear. But first, I wanted to show you . . . *this.*"

She pushed the doors open and gestured for Andy and Mika to walk in first. As soon as Andy stepped inside the giant room, all thoughts of *OlympiFan* and the Masked Medalist temporarily fled his mind.

Row after row of tables were covered in giant computer monitors and all kinds of equipment. The screens were showing different Olympic events, and everyone sitting behind a computer wore large headphones. More people milled up and down the rows, swiping tablets or talking on their phones.

"Wow," Mika breathed as they walked slowly down a row, watching all the different events playing on the monitors.

"I've never seen so many screens in my entire life," Andy said.

Mom looked pleased. "More than a thousand screens, as a matter of fact! Every television network in the world broadcasting the Games to their home countries does it from right here. Pretty cool, huh?"

"*Very* cool!" Andy tried to imagine how many people were watching the Olympics all over the world right now. The thought made his head spin.

After their tour, Mom took Andy and Mika to a giant cafeteria. They grabbed trays and joined the line at the hot dish area. "Have you two had *katsudon* yet?" Mom asked.

"Yeah, at that place in Little Tokyo in LA!" Andy replied.

"It's one of my favorites," added Mika.

Mom gave the woman behind the counter her order, and then turned to Andy and Mika with a grin. "I meant *here* in Tokyo, goofballs."

"Oh." Andy grinned. "Nope, not yet!"

The woman reappeared with three big bowls and three small bowls, and Andy felt his stomach rumble as he accepted one of each. The bigger bowl was filled with rice topped with strips of fried pork cutlet, sautéed onions, and a beaten egg cooked in broth, while the smaller bowl contained grated carrots and some sort of white vegetable. As Mom led them through the crowded cafeteria, Andy looked around at all of the faces. He heard people speaking in English and Japanese, Spanish and Russian, and more languages that he might've been able to guess if the cafeteria hadn't been so noisy.

Mom found a table where her Compete reporters were already eating. They both looked up and smiled at Andy and Mika as they sat down.

"You guys remember James and Valentina, right?" Mom asked.

"Yes! Hi," said Andy.

"Hello!" Mika sat down next to Andy and pulled apart her chopsticks. *"Mmm,"* she said, taking a big bite of pork and rice.

Valentina laughed. "Are you two loving the food in Tokyo?"

"Definitely," Andy said, digging into his bowl. "We even had octopus."

"Ah, was it takoyaki?" James asked, and Andy nodded. "I had that for a snack yesterday!"

Mika swallowed, then took a bite from the other bowl. "So this is carrots, and . . . what's the other thing?"

"It's called *daikon*," Mom told her. "It's a type of radish. That's a carrot and *daikon namasu*—a raw salad marinated in sweetened vinegar."

"Have you two managed to collect any pins yet?" Valentina asked.

Andy looked up. "Pins?" he repeated.

"Yeah!" She pointed to her vest, and Andy saw six colorful pins. Two looked like variations of the Compete logo, but he didn't recognize the others.

"Emma had pins like that!" Mika exclaimed. "Can we buy them somewhere?"

"Hang on. They don't know about the pins?" Valentina gave Mom a look of mock horror.

Mom laughed. "Want to explain it to them?"

"For sure." Valentina tucked a stray light brown curl behind her ear and smiled at Andy and Mika. "So pin trading is *a really big deal* at the Olympics. Anyone can make a pin—you'll see them for teams, media, other companies, and sponsors—and they're always unique to that year's Games. They're serious collector's items. Really rare pins from past Olympics can sell for hundreds or even thousands of dollars."

Andy's eyes widened. "Jeez. And people trade them here?"

"Yep. James had these made for us." Valentina

gestured to the two Compete pins on her vest. "I took a bunch and bartered with vendors and random people I've met for the other pins—a PyeongChang 2018, two Tokyo tourism boards, and this one from that sportswear company, what are they called? Ah—Enspire."

Suddenly, Mika started to choke on her katsudon. She reached for her water, coughing loudly, then took a giant sip.

"Are you okay, honey?" Mom asked, leaning around Andy and patting her on the back.

"Yeah!" Mika's voice was slightly hoarse, but she nodded vigorously. Her face was tomato red, and Andy noticed she kept shooting little glances at Valentina's pins. "Totally fine."

"You two should definitely start collecting." Valentina elbowed James's arm. "Let's help them out, shall we?"

"Of course!" James produced a small bag from under the table, unzipped the front pocket, and pulled out a plastic pouch filled with different pins. He gave a handful each to Andy and Mika. "All right, Kudo kids, you've gotta wear at least one of the Compete pins for the rest of the Games. Promote your mom," he said with a wink, and they laughed.

"Thank you!" Andy pinned one to his shirt, then stuck the rest in his pocket. He couldn't help noticing that his sister was still blushing. He waited until Mom, Valentina, and James were deep in conversation about work, then nudged Mika's arm with his elbow.

"What's going on?"

"Huh? Nothing!" Mika said, examining her pins. "Ooh, this one looks like a butterfly. See?"

She held out the pink pin, her expression completely innocent. But she wasn't fooling Andy one bit, and he gave her a pointed look to let her know it. Mika was incapable of keeping secrets, especially from him, so Andy wasn't too annoyed. Whatever it was, she'd tell him soon enough.

In the meantime, Andy had more than enough puzzles to focus on: finding the Silver medal and discovering who'd left that note. For the hundredth time that day, Andy pictured the mysterious creator of *OlympiFan* lurking in the trees near the Meiji Shrine, watching all of the players, and leaving a special clue for just one of them to find.

It was ridiculous, of course. But Andy couldn't help but think, *What if?*

OLYMPIFAN UPDATE!
Special message from the Masked Medalist

Hello, OlympiFans! BIG congratulations to
Team Cryptic on their Bronze medal win!
That was a close race—which just makes
the game more fun, don't you think?

If you're checking the scoreboard, you probably
know that Team Cryptic opted for 250 points
and two hints to my identity.

What would your team have chosen—more hints,
or more points? Better figure that out,
because **YOU** just might find the Silver!

In the meantime, I'll be cheering for all of the divers
and swimmers competing this afternoon!
Which events are you most excited about?

CHAPTER TEN

RJ: OMG. Almost 50 comments! 😄😄😄

MK: I KNOW. 😄🎉

RJ: And that one you posted a few hours ago already has 20 comments!

MK: I. KNOW.

RJ: Where'd you meet that lady with all the pins in the picture?

MK: At the diving event! Her name's Sandra. This was her twelfth time coming to the Olympics. 😮

RJ: WHOA. I guess that's why she had so many of those pins?

MK: Yeah! She even swapped with me. I gave her a Compete pin and she gave me one from Athens 2004!!

RJ: That's so cool!

RJ: Are you still going to delete your account when you come home?

MK: Yup. I think I have to.

RJ: ☹️☹️☹️

MK: My parents would be SO MAD if they knew I had one even for this contest! Besides, what would I post after Tokyo anyway?

RJ: Ummm . . . there are plenty of pretty things to take pictures of in LA, tyvm

MK: LOL

RJ: And you're good at taking pictures.

RJ: You could be a professional photographer, like that documentary guy said.

RJ: And Instagram lets you show off your pics to a ton of people and maybe even get sponsors and stuff. And the first thing you ever posted got a comment from a big famous company and might even be featured in a freaking commercial!!!!!

RJ: BUT WHATEVER, NO REASON TO KEEP YOUR ACCOUNT OR ANYTHING 😑

MK: OKAY FIIINE LOL. But that won't change my parents' minds.

RJ: ☹

MK: Ok, gotta go. 😔

RJ: 👍 ☺

RJ: Lily, Po & Turtle say goodnight!

Mika grinned when a photo popped up. Lily and Po were both curled up like two fluffy white balls on the sofa next to Riley. Behind them, Turtle the beagle sat on the rug, giving the two puppies a disdainful look. Riley's mom had a strict humans-only-on-the-couch rule, but clearly Lily and Po hadn't quite learned to follow it yet. Or maybe they *had* learned, and they just didn't care.

She closed her messages, then glanced over at the other twin bed. Andy was already sound asleep, mouth wide open with his arms and legs splayed out over the entire bed. From the other side of the door, Mika could faintly hear the sound of Dad's snores.

Her eyelids felt heavy, but she couldn't resist checking the comments for the photo Riley had been talking about one more time before going to sleep. After lunch, Mom had taken her and Andy to watch the diving event. Mika had been captivated by every single diver; no matter how long she watched, each time they leapt off the board, she felt as if her heart was trying to jump up into her mouth. She'd been tempted to try and get another photo of someone in the crowd, but she was too nervous that Mom or someone from Compete would notice.

Then Mika had gone to find the restroom, and she'd met Sandra.

She was older than Mika's parents, with gray hair that frizzed in the humidity and warm brown eyes behind turquoise-framed glasses. Mika had spotted her standing against a wall featuring a beautiful mural of all the Olympic water sports. A small crowd had gathered around the woman, many of them taking her photo, and it was easy to see why. She wore a long, flowing skirt, a loose tank top, a giant floppy straw hat, and almost every square inch of clothing was covered in Olympic pins.

"And these are just the ones I'm here to trade," she'd said with a wink. "The really valuable ones are pinned to a much more expensive hat."

That had gotten a big laugh, and Mika hadn't been able to resist stopping to take a photo, too. She moved to the other side of the crowd for a better angle. The woman had done a little twirl, pins rattling as her skirt billowed around her. She'd beamed as Mika had taken the picture, then spotted the pins on Mika's shirt.

"Ooh! Looking to trade?"

"Sure!" Mika stepped forward, taking off one of her Compete pins and handing it over. Her eyes flicked to the small sign next to the woman.

SWAP WITH SANDRA!
Over two thousand pins collected from 12 Olympic Games

Sandra had taken the pin. "Compete! Lovely. Do you have a preference?" She did a little shake, causing her pins to rattle again. Mika giggled and shook her head. "Well then, how about . . ." Tapping her finger to her chin, Sandra gazed down at her pins for a few seconds. "This one!" she decided, removing a pin from the neckline of her top. She handed it to Mika, then attached the Compete pin in the same spot. "The Olympics started in ancient Greece, you know. Almost two thousand eight hundred years ago!"

"Wow," Mika breathed, examining her new pin. It was a coliseum filled with people in a rainbow of colors, and ATHENS 2004 was printed at the bottom. She loved it. "Thank you so much!"

"Pleasure doing business with you!" Sandra replied as Mika hurried off.

She posted the photo of Sandra on Instagram before she returned from the restroom. By the time Mom took her and Andy to meet Dad for dinner, it had gotten more than thirty comments.

Mika wiggled her feet happily under the covers as she read the latest comments. The photo of Sandra had come out really well—her coy little smile as she looked right at the camera, the way the lights glinted off her pins, her skirt midtwirl. It was even better than her first photo!

A new notification popped up, but not a like or a comment—a direct message. Mika opened it, her confusion quickly turning to fear as she read.

> **A_Fan:** Do your parents know what a talented photographer their daughter is?

Mika sat up straight in bed. She tapped on A_Fan's blank avatar, which brought her to the person's page. No posts, no followers. Whoever it was, maybe this person created an account just to send Mika this message?

Her hands went cold and clammy, and her heart started racing. Someone out there knew this was Mika's account. The message was complimentary, but the more Mika thought about it, the more her guilt led her to feel like it was a threat. This person wanted her to know that they could tell her parents her secret.

Mika glanced over at Andy, still splayed out like a starfish on his bed. She started to throw her comforter off so she could wake him up. If she showed this message to her brother, maybe it wouldn't seem so scary. Then she froze, one leg dangling off her bed. Mika really, really wanted to show Andy the message, but that would mean telling him about her Instagram account. She'd never kept such a big secret from him, and she didn't like it.

But Andy might make her show their parents this

message from A_Fan, and they would have her delete the account for sure. Her photos had so many comments— and Enspire had already noticed her! Mika really believed she had a good chance at getting picked to be part of their campaign. Plus, it was just so much *fun*. She loved taking photos, she loved editing them, and she loved all the praise they got once they were posted.

Taking a deep breath, Mika looked at the message from A_Fan again. Then she closed the app, plugged her phone in to charge, and curled up under the comforter. Just because someone knew this was her account didn't mean they were threatening her. Besides, what reason would they even have to get her in trouble with her parents? It didn't make any sense. Maybe the person was just trying to compliment her and didn't realize how creepy it came across.

Still, it was a long time before Mika was able to fall asleep.

OLYMPIFAN UPDATE!
Locations for the Silver Medal

So many clues, so little time . . . I hope you OlympiFans
are ready for more exploring!

Whether you're playing in VR or AR mode, I'm sure
you've realized by now that Tokyo is **HUGE**.
Get ready to discover even more of it over
the next few days! Head to these locations
to find clues for the Silver medal:

Ueno
Fujimi
Ginza
Shiodome
Higashi-Shinbashi

Happy clue hunting, OlympiFans!

CHAPTER ELEVEN
ANDY

THE MOMENT MIKA'S alarm went off, Andy swiped uselessly at the nightstand. His head felt thick and groggy with sleep, and he wondered blearily how long jet lag lasted. All he wanted was to sink back into his dreams. He'd been swimming . . . he'd been *racing*. Backstroke, butter-fly, freestyle—slicing through the water, the other competitors barely visible in his peripheral vision.

But he had to wake up, because something exciting was happening this morning. Something he was looking forward to. What was it?

"Wake up, Andy! We've got clues to find," Mika announced, and Andy felt a jolt of adrenaline shock him awake. His sister snickered as he struggled to sit up and rub his eyes. "Wow, I've never seen you wake up this fast before. It's kind of scary. Like a zombie jumping out of a grave or something."

Ignoring this, Andy grabbed his phone and opened *OlympiFan*. Still rubbing his eyes, he stifled a huge yawn and navigated to the Team MADR chat room. Devon had left a message just an hour earlier:

> **Devon:** Can you guys get to the zoo? The VR line is already pretty long 😞

The previous night, Mom and Dad had taken Andy and Mika to dinner at a sushi restaurant with James and Valentina. While the adults had talked over platters of sushi and sashimi, the Kudo kids had come up with a plan. They'd shared the mysterious message in the note with Devon and Riley, and all four had agreed that the most obvious interpretation of "pandas guard the Silver" was that the medal was hidden at a zoo—and Ueno Zoo was the only one in the city. When the locations for clues to the Silver had been released and Ueno had been one of the five, Andy wasn't sure what to think. Could it just be a coincidence? Or was this really a clue from the Masked Medalist that only Team MADR knew about?

Because the zoo was too far away from their hotel to walk and Andy and Mika weren't sure how to get there by train, Devon and Riley were going to check it out in VR mode while Andy and Mika searched for clues in a location closer to their hotel. But apparently, that wasn't going to work since the VR line was already so long.

Andy glanced over at Mika, who was sitting cross-legged on her bed, gazing intently at her phone. "Should we do it?"

Mika looked up sharply, dropping her phone into her lap. "Should we do what?"

"What Devon said." Andy paused, fighting off another yawn. "Go to the zoo, see if the Silver's there. Aren't you on *OlympiFan?*"

"Oh!" Mika blinked. "Yeah, I was. I am. I mean, I was about to open it." She picked her phone up and angled it slightly away from Andy as she swiped. "But I don't know if the Silver would even be in the same location with the clues. There weren't any clues around the shrine, just the Bronze."

Before Andy could respond, someone knocked on their door.

"We're awake!" called Mika, and a moment later, Dad poked his head in. His eyebrows raised at the sight of Andy sitting up in bed.

"You're *both* up?" he said in disbelief. "Mika, what did you do, throw cold water on him?"

"He actually woke up *when the alarm went off,*" Mika said, matching Dad's tone of mock amazement.

Andy rolled his eyes as Dad pretended to clutch his heart.

"Just wanted to let you guys know that I'm taking the morning off!" Dad went on, stepping inside their room. "Emi called a meeting after lunch, but until then, I'm up for anything. What do you guys want to do?"

Andy and Mika glanced at one another, a quick,

silent conversation. Mika lifted a shoulder, and Andy nodded once. They both turned back to Dad, who looked from one to the other expectantly. "So?"

Andy tried to keep his voice light. "Can we check out the zoo?"

While Dad stood in line for tickets, Andy and Mika huddled together near the entrance. It wasn't even ten o'clock yet, but the sun was already blazing hot. Andy could feel sweat beading on his forehead, while Mika kept glancing around nervously.

"Who are you looking for?" Andy finally asked.

She blinked. "What?"

"You look like you're looking for someone."

"Well . . ." Mika hesitated. "It's just weird, you know? Whoever left the note at the gate was probably watching us. Maybe they're here too, watching to see if we find the Silver."

"It's not going to be here." Andy paused before adding quietly, "At least, I hope it's not."

Mika stared at him. "What? Why not?"

Andy had been thinking about this during the whole train ride to the zoo. "Because if it *is* here, and we find the medal and get all those points and the hints about the Masked Medalist's identity, then we cheated."

"*Cheated?*"

"Yeah! We haven't collected enough clues to figure out where the Silver is."

"If the Silver really is here, then that note *was* a clue!"

"But it wasn't an official *OlympiFan* clue."

"Unless the Masked Medalist left it."

"Why would they do that, though?" Andy insisted. "It's not only unfair to the VR players, like you said yesterday—it's also unfair to everyone who wasn't at that gate at the right time. Remember, in this game you're supposed to work with your team and respect the other players. This is just . . ." Andy paused, trying to find the right word. "It's not good sportsmanship. I don't think it's something the Masked Medalist would do."

Mika chewed her lip. "Okay, I see your point. But if the Silver medal *is* here, are we just going to leave it?"

Andy didn't answer. That was the question he kept going back and forth on. If he was going to be a beta tester for the Masked Medalist's new gaming company, he needed to figure out their identity. And to do that, he needed at least one of the hints that came with the medals. He didn't want to cheat; he wanted to solve the puzzle and win the right way.

If the Silver medal really was waiting right inside, would Andy actually be able to resist claiming it? Could he pass up the chance at claiming two hints to the Masked Medalist's identity for his team?

"Got 'em!" Dad appeared, waving three tickets.

"This was a great idea, guys. I needed to get outdoors after spending so much time in the business center on my laptop."

Andy smiled weakly as they headed to the entrance. On the other side, Dad stopped at a kiosk to grab a map, which he unfolded with gusto.

"Directly ahead, we've got Japanese birds on the left, and—*ooh* . . . giant pandas on the right!"

Andy felt a fresh wave of anxiety.

"Pandas!" Mika said quickly, grinning at Dad. "Let's go!"

Dozens of people were already milling around in front of the panda exhibit. Behind the giant glass wall, Andy could see two of the enormous, cuddly-looking bears. One was taking a nap while the other contentedly stripped the leaves from a long piece of bamboo. Dad and Mika made their way to the front of the crowd, Andy trailing behind them, phone out and ready. He opened *OlympiFan* and entered AR mode, holding his breath.

The footprints were blue.

Andy scanned the exhibit through the screen, the knot in his stomach slowly loosening. The only thing that popped up was one of the game's little "fun fact" bubbles:

Did you know pandas have six digits per paw?
Five fingers and one thumb!

For the first time that morning, Andy felt himself start to relax. The Silver medal wasn't here. Whoever had left the note had been wrong.

Not *wrong*, he realized suddenly. Because that person *had* known where the Bronze medal would be. Which meant they were *lying*. They'd wanted to mislead someone on purpose with that note.

But why?

1st		Cryptic	453
2nd		夢	221
3rd		The Oracles	219
4th		SuperFan	203
5th		Majestic Turmoil	197
6th		Dragonflame	195
7th		геймеров	192
8th		흰 호랑이	190
9th		Rabenklaue	188
10th		ALLEYOOP	187

CHAPTER TWELVE

MIKA

MIKA BREATHED A sigh of relief as they left the panda exhibit. She hadn't thought about it before, but Andy was right—if they'd actually found the Silver, it would have been cheating to claim the medal. Or at least, it wouldn't have been fair to the other players. That was pretty much the definition of cheating, right?

They wandered past an information center, heading over to the exhibit of Japanese birds. Mika leaned closer to Andy. "Kind of weird that the VR line was so long, isn't it?" she whispered. "Part of me thought the Silver really was here, and a bunch of players had already figured it out."

Andy shrugged. "I think it's just because Ueno was on the list of locations. Plus, you know—the zoo is a cool place to visit. Better in real life than virtual reality, though," he added with a grin.

Mika laughed. "That's true." She noticed tiny blue footprints visible at the bottom of Andy's screen. "Oh, right . . . guess I should look for clues, too!"

She pulled out her phone just as Dad lowered the map. "Apparently there's a pagoda right over here," he said, pointing to a path next to the bird exhibit. "Let's check that out first!"

Mika and Andy hurried after him, still scanning for clues through their screens. When they stepped into a clearing, Mika looked up and stared in amazement. The pagoda was much bigger than she'd expected—five stories tall, each tier featuring intricate carvings and ceramic designs. She held up her phone again.

"'Kaneiji is a Buddhist temple that was first built in 1631,'" she read, and Dad turned to look at her.

"How'd you know that?"

"*OlympiFan*," she explained, showing him the fact bubble that had popped up on her screen.

"Ah, yes." Dad's expression cleared. "Andy showed me that feature. I have to admit . . . that's pretty cool . . . for a game."

His tone was teasing, and Mika smiled. She turned, expecting Andy to say something defensive—but he was hurrying toward the pagoda, eyes on his screen.

"What's he . . . oh!" Mika gasped. "Look, Dad—the footprints are yellow!"

"What's that mean?" Dad asked, but she was already running after Andy. Her eyes stayed glued to the footprints, which glowed brighter and brighter. She and Andy both slowed as they drew closer to the pagoda, and after a few seconds, Mika's footprints turned pink.

"Over here!"

She spotted the tiny, fluttering animation just as Andy and Dad reached her. "It's a music note!" Mika told Dad, tapping the clue. Team MADR had collected a few dozen last night. A moment later, her screen went black, and her phone emitted a short, chirp-like sound. Then the clue collection page opened, and she saw the single music note.

"It's a sound clip," Andy explained when Dad leaned closer to look. "So the more we collect, the longer the clip."

"I thought the clues were colors?" Dad asked.

"That was for the Bronze," Mika explained. "They were actually pixels from a photo."

"The game has language settings, but the clues don't use words," Andy added. "The Masked Medalist said it's so that no one's at a disadvantage because of a bad translation or something like that."

Dad looked impressed. "Actually, that's pretty clever."

They collected more clues as they explored the zoo. Mika's favorite exhibit by far was the Aye-Aye Forest, a dark cluster of trees with tiny creatures that looked like a mix between bats and monkeys hanging from the branches. While Dad and Andy started to head toward the okapis, Mika lingered a few steps behind, watching one particularly tiny aye-aye on a low-hanging branch tapping on the wood. Her eyes had finally adjusted to the darkness of the exhibit, and she could see just how long and skinny the aye-aye's fingers were. Another aye-aye shifted around in the tree, black eyes glinting as it stared curiously at Mika. She couldn't decide whether the animals were cute or scary, but if the souvenir shop sold any stuffed aye-ayes, she was definitely getting one. She snapped a photo to send to Riley, then hurried to catch up with Dad and Andy.

When Mika stepped out of the exhibit, she had to shade her eyes against the sunlight. She could see Dad and Andy standing just outside of the enormous metal fence surrounding the okapis, which looked a little like a horse but with zebra legs. Mika took out her phone, intent on opening *OlympiFan* to see if any clues were nearby.

Almost without her permission, her fingers swiped over to the Instagram icon instead.

Mika had woken up thinking about A_Fan's message. She hadn't wanted to open Instagram because she was scared that another message would be waiting. But spending the morning at the zoo with Dad and Andy had helped ease her fear. Just because someone had figured out she had an account didn't mean they were threatening her.

And she really wanted to see how many likes her posts were up to.

Holding her breath, Mika opened the app. She exhaled with relief; there were lots of new likes and comments, but no new messages. Scrolling through the comments on the photo of Sandra, Mika walked slowly toward the okapi exhibit. She'd only taken a few steps when a tiny *1* popped up in the top right-hand corner. Mika stopped in her tracks and opened the direct message.

> **A_Fan:** No luck with the pandas? Too bad.

A chill raced up Mika's neck despite the heat. She turned in a circle, staring around wildly as realization dawned. A_Fan knew about the pandas . . . *they must have left the note.* But they couldn't have known exactly when Mika would go to the zoo, or even if she would.

Unless they were *watching* her.

TEAM SUPERFAN CHAT ROOM

SabineTheGreat: Okay, team! SuperZuki proposed a new game strategy yesterday. Let's make it official by recording our votes here in our chat room. All those in favor of the new strategy, respond to this thread with Y. All those opposed, respond with N.

SuperZuki: Y

AgentAngel: N

DragonmasterMolly: N

IronMatt: N

AquaMaria: N

CaptainArmando: N

SuperZuki: Fine.

SuperZuki: I guess you guys aren't serious about winning.

TEAM DRAGONFLAME CHAT ROOM

MageMisaki: Well, the zoo was a total bust.☹

CentaurCici: What are you talking about?! You found 46 clues!

MageMisaki: I'm not talking about the clues.

GoblinGeorge: Ummm I just found something interesting.

GoblinGeorge: You know Tamrel the Terrible? On Dragon Blaze?

CentaurCici: No, I'm totally unfamiliar with the all-time best player on the all-time best online game that I play literally every day of my life. 😊

GoblinGeorge: Ha ha.

GoblinGeorge: Well, Tamrel is Tobias Malavia. Argentinean boxer—won a bunch of medals. I just downloaded his video from the Gallery and he talked about playing Dragon Blaze!!!

CentaurCici: WHOA

TEAM GHOSTCADETS CHAT ROOM

CadetRicky: Guys. Even the guy making a documentary about OlympiFan thinks Chiang Li is the Masked Medalist. I TOLD YOU.

CadetJames: He does????

CadetMadison: No, he said other players think it's Chiang! He didn't say HE thinks it's Chiang!

CadetKara: ^^true. But still interesting that other players think so . . . hmm.

CadetJames: I wonder if Team Cryptic thinks it's Chiang? They're the only ones with the hints so far!

CadetRicky: IT'S CHIANG, OK

CHAPTER THIRTEEN
ANDY

DP: TilerMyths has over 400 clues now. By himself. His team has 426.

DP: HOW?!?

AK: IDK.

DP: Maybe he's cheating.

DP: WAIT. What if he left that note about the pandas??

AK: ???

DP: Because you were so close! Maybe it was to distract you or something!

AK: But anyone could have found it. Mika just happened to see it first.

AK: Also he was playing VR, remember? He wasn't there.

DP: Oh yeah

DP: His teammate??

AK: UppeRcase is barely playing! Only collected 26 clues.

AK: If they win the silver, it won't matter who gets the gold. Tiler will have four hints. He'll probably be able to guess who the MM is.

DP: Any ideas what the sound clips mean?

AK: Not yet. All I hear are bells, and maybe a whistle 😬

DP: Yeah same.

DP: Uh oh, Mom's coming. If she catches me on my phone after 11 she'll take it away 💀

DP: BYE

Andy gazed absentmindedly at his screen. The idea that TilerMyths might have left the note had made his stomach leap for a moment. After all, Devon's theory about it being a strategy to distract Andy and slow down their team made sense. But whoever had left the note was obviously in Tokyo, and TilerMyths only played in VR mode.

Wait.

Andy stood abruptly. Across the lobby, the elevator

doors opened and Mika stepped out. She hurried over, patting her backpack.

"I can't believe I almost left without this," she said before seeing the look on his face. "What's wrong?"

"What if TilerMyths left the note?" Andy said, thinking out loud. "This whole time, we were thinking that just because he's playing VR means he's not here. But he could be here. He could be here in Tokyo and he just never plays in AR mode."

Mika's face had gone pale. "Why would he do that?"

"As a strategy." Andy was speaking faster now. "Think about it. He was there at the park, racing to get to the medal just like the rest of us. But he won in VR mode. Then he left that note about the zoo to throw us off."

"But how would he even know I'd find it?"

"You and I weren't the only *OlympiFan* players there," Andy pointed out. "The whole SuperFan team was there, probably some other players, too; he knew there was a good chance that a player who'd come close to winning the Bronze would find that note."

"But that note was meant for me!"

Andy stared at his sister, noticing for the first time how frightened she looked. "What? Why do you think that?"

"Because he . . ." Mika glanced away, pressing her lips together. "I don't know. I just feel like he knew I would find it."

Once again, Andy had the feeling his sister wasn't telling him something. But before he could say anything else, Mom emerged from the conference room at the end of the lobby, followed by Hana Takahashi and Wesley Brooks. "You guys ready?" Mom asked cheerfully as she approached, and Andy and Mika nodded.

They took the train to the Olympic Stadium, where track-and-field events were going on all day. Hana seemed a bit distracted and quiet today, but Wesley chatted briefly with Andy and Mika, asking them about which events they'd watched so far and what kinds of things they'd done in Tokyo.

"How was the zoo?" Wesley asked. "We haven't had a chance to do any fun touristy stuff yet!"

"It was great." Andy paused, expecting Mika to chime in, but she seemed unusually subdued. "The okapis were my favorite. Oh, and we found thirty-one clues! For *OlympiFan*," he added quickly.

"Nice!" Wesley said. "Still having fun with that game?"

"Yeah, it's awesome." Andy almost told Wesley about his close call with the Bronze medal, then stopped. That just made him think about the note, and Andy didn't want to talk about the real reason he and Mika had gone to the zoo. He still felt a rush of guilt every time he thought about it.

"I was never any good at puzzles," Wesley said. "But I used to play *Dragon Blaze*—it's one of those online role-playing games."

"Yeah, I've heard of it!" Andy replied eagerly. "Were you good?"

Wesley shrugged modestly. "I wasn't too bad. That's actually how Hana and I got to be friends." He lowered his voice as their train slowed to a halt. "Her character's name was Anah the Huntress."

"Really?" Andy asked Hana. In response, she pretended to hold a bow and arrow like an archer, her brow scrunched in mock concentration, and he laughed. "Nice name."

Hana lowered her arms and grinned. "You have to admit, it's much cooler than Sir Somer the Salty."

"Hey," Wesley said defensively. "It's gymnastics-related! I thought it was clever . . ."

Andy chuckled, then glanced at Mika. She was gazing at an ad over the subway doors, her expression distant. Andy was starting to worry about his sister, but he didn't want to ask her what was going on in front of Mom.

He never got a chance at the event, either. Because moments after they entered the arena, Mika said, "Oh look, there's Emma!"

Andy and Mom turned to look past rows of spectators. Finally, Andy spotted a familiar-looking girl with curly black hair standing next to a woman who Andy guessed was her mother. Both of them wore yellow-and-green jerseys, each clutching an end of a bright yellow banner that read WE LOVE YOU, ANTONY! in giant green letters.

"Oh yeah!" Mika turned to Mom, grabbing her arm. "We met her at the Meiji Shrine—she told us her brother's competing today! Can we go say hi to her, pretty please?"

Andy thought his sister looked ready to pull out the pitiful sheep bleating if necessary. But Mom was already smiling.

"I think that would be nice! Meet me right here after the event, okay? And make sure to text me if you need anything."

"Thanks, Mom!" Andy and Mika chorused before racing up the steps. Overhead, a deep voice boomed over the intercom, introducing the hurdlers.

"From Jamaica, Tion Alwood. From Cuba, Marco Alvarez. From Canada, Jason Kim. From South Africa, Antony Botha. From Kenya, Chege Mutahi . . ."

"Emma! Hi!" Mika exclaimed, and Emma whirled around. For just a second, an odd expression crossed her face. But it was gone a moment later, and Emma beamed at them.

"Oh! Mika, Andy! Hi!" Emma sounded ready to burst with excitement. "Mom, these are some friends I made the other day, when I went to the shrine, remember?"

"Hello! You two have perfect timing," Emma's mother said with a broad smile. "Our Antony is about to show everyone what he's made of!"

"Which one is he?" Andy asked eagerly, staring down at the men now taking their places on the track.

Emma pointed. "Third from the left," she said, and Andy spotted him in green-and-yellow shorts and a tank top.

A hush fell over the crowd as the men crouched, heads

bowed, waiting. Suddenly the atmosphere was almost un-bearably tense, and Andy found himself wondering what it was like to have that many eyes on you—not just here in the stadium, but all of those cameras broadcasting your performance to countless people around the entire world. Was Antony thinking about that right now? Probably not, Andy decided. He was too focused on the race.

Bang! At the sound of the shot, the athletes sprang forward while cheers erupted from the crowd. Andy watched as the athletes leapt over the first, second, and third hurdles in almost perfect unison, marveling at their speed. At the fifth hurdle, a few competitors started to pull ahead, including Antony. By the eighth, two run-ners surged in front of the pack, hurdling over the last two and crossing the finish line at practically the same time. Antony followed barely a second later, the rest of the athletes not far behind him.

The crowd roared as the announcer's voice boomed throughout the stadium. Emma and her mother jumped up and down, screaming and cheering, as Antony slowed to a jog. Even from here, Andy could see the grin on his face. Antony had just won a bronze medal!

"Yes! Go, Antony!" Mika hollered, jumping up and down just like Emma and her mom. Andy cheered too, amazed at what he'd just witnessed. He laughed as Emma slung her arm around Mika in a half hug, nearly tripping over the backs of the seats in the next row in their enthusiasm. He was relieved to see his sister acting like her normal, happy self again. Maybe he'd been worried about nothing. If something was *really* wrong, Mika wouldn't keep it a secret from him.

After the track-and-field events, Emma and her mother were in a hurry to see Antony. "We should hang out later, though!" Emma said, still beaming from ear to ear after her brother's performance. "Text me, okay?"

"I will!" Mika promised.

Mom walked Andy and Mika out of the stadium, where Dad met them. The three of them said goodbye to Mom, then took a taxi to Hamarikyu Gardens in the Shiodome district. There was a library nearby that Dad had wanted to visit for research, so Andy and Mika were going to search for clues while he worked. After going over the rules one more time, Dad waved and headed into the library while Andy and Mika walked to the gardens and started to search.

Andy spotted a clue at the edge of the pond, quickly adding it to the rest of the sound clips. This one was a little *tick-tick* sound. Hamarikyu Gardens was turning out to be loaded with clues—they'd already found a dozen in just under an hour. The first one he'd found had been a low, almost supersonic-sounding *boom* that was barely audible through his phone's tiny speakers.

Andy spotted a bench by the water. "Let's take a break for a sec. We should try listening to our sound clips again."

The siblings sat down and plugged in their earbuds. Andy nodded, and they both hit *play* on their phones at the same time.

Listening intently, Andy frowned. The clip was maybe ten seconds long so far. But it still sounded like a random collection of sounds: tinkling bells, a shrill whistle, that cannon-like *boom*, and the new *tick-tick*. He played it three times in a row, then pulled out his earbuds and sighed.

"I *still* have no idea."

Mika was listening for a fourth time, brow furrowed. "You know what this reminds me of?" she said slowly. "That cuckoo clock Aunt Kei has. That last one you added really sounds like a clock ticking, plus hers plays that melody that sounds kind of like the bells."

Andy stared at her. "You're right. But what about the low noise? The one that sounds like a cannon?"

"Ugh, I have no idea. Maybe it's a gigantic clock? Like Big Ben?"

She sounded like she was joking, but Andy opened his browser anyway. "Giant . . . clock . . . Tokyo . . ." he murmured as he typed, and Mika giggled.

"Pretty sure if Tokyo had a Big Ben, Dad would've put it on our list of places to see."

Andy had to admit that she had a point, but when the search results popped up, his mouth fell open.

"Mika, look—this has to be it!"

Ten minutes later, Andy and Mika raced out of the park. "It's just a few blocks this way!" Andy called, dodging around a group of kids wearing tiny backpacks. He pictured himself as an Olympic athlete leaping effortlessly over hurdles, darting around barriers, and sprinting toward the Silver.

But when Andy turned onto the street where the Giant Ghibli Clock waited, a bunch of avatars appeared on his screen, and he groaned. Already, at least a dozen other players were heading to the clock—CadetRicky and CadetKara were coming in from the other direction, Shellbee, Beeyanca, and Feebee weren't far behind Andy and Mika, and a half a block ahead, right in front of the clock . . . SabineTheGreat.

Team SuperFan was already there.

"Hurry!" Andy cried as he and Mika put on a fresh burst of speed. But it was too late. Before they even reached the clock, the message popped up on their screens.

Found by SabineTheGreat (VR)

**Congratulations to the Silver Medalists:
TEAM SUPERFAN!!!**

Andy slowed to a stop, gasping for breath as Mika came to a halt next to him. They exchanged matching looks of disbelief. How could they have come so close only to lose at the last second *again*?

Pedestrians were craning their necks, staring at the group of teens screaming and jumping up and down in celebration. Andy tore his gaze from them and looked at the clock. It really was cool—a massive copper-and-steel structure at least three stories high. On either side of the clockface were little balconies and doors opening and closing to reveal tiny cannons, miniature blacksmiths hammering away, whistling teapots, and lots of spinning gears and cranking pistons.

Mika sighed. "I'm going to take some photos."

While she crossed the street, Andy opened the Team MADR chat room.

> **Andy:** So close AGAIN. It was at the Giant Ghibli Clock. We got there two seconds after Team SuperFan. ☹

> **Andy:** At least TilerMyths didn't win this time. His team already has two hints.

Sticking his phone in his pocket, Andy looked back at Team SuperFan. While they'd mostly stopped screaming, one guy was still jumping up and down and chanting something as the others laughed.

Suddenly, Mika reappeared. "Andy, look," she said

urgently, showing him her phone. Andy glanced down at the photo of Team SuperFan.

"That's from the Meiji Shrine," he said, frowning.

"Yes, but *look*." Mika jabbed her finger at the screen, and Andy looked more closely. The group of teens was centered in the picture, all staring glumly at their screens. But not far behind them, Gavin Driscoll stood with his giant camera, interviewing the sullen-looking boy with the huge sunglasses that took up half his face. His camera was aimed at the boy, who was clearly talking, but Gavin's head was turned toward Mika, as if he were looking at something just to her left. Andy thought about where they'd been standing, and his head snapped up.

"Gavin's looking at the spot where you found the note?"

Mika nodded. "I think so. He was there. Do you think he's the one who left it?"

Andy stared hard at the photo again, hoping to spot something he'd missed. "I guess it's possible . . . but why would he do that?"

"He's making a documentary about *OlympiFan*," Mika said. "Maybe he thought this would make it more dramatic or something."

Andy shook his head slowly. "I don't know, that'd be pretty extreme."

Mika looked unsettled. But after a moment, she

nodded. "Yeah, you're right. I still think it's kinda weird, though."

Andy had to agree. Someone was trying to disrupt the game.

But even that wasn't as weird as Mika's behavior. During the whole walk back to the library, she kept glancing over her shoulder, as if she thought she was being followed. Every time Andy tried to ask her why she was acting so nervous, she'd brush him off. By the time they met up with Dad, Andy was starting to get a little annoyed with his sister.

Then again, she didn't have to tell him. Technically, it was none of his business, anyway.

He already had enough mysteries to solve.

OLYMPIFAN UPDATE!

Special message from the Masked Medalist

Hey there, OlympiFans! BIG congrats to Team SuperFan on finding the Silver medal at the Giant Ghibli Clock— what an exciting race! By the way, how cool is that clock? It was designed by Hayao Miyazaki, for all you anime fangirls and fanboys out there. Including me.

(Wait, was that a hint? Whoops!
Consider it a freebie . . .)

As you've probably noticed, Team SuperFan went all in on the points—750—bringing their total to a whopping 1,021!!! They also received one hint to my identity and immediate access to the locations for the Gold medal.

The locations will be up for everyone else in one hour. In the meantime, I don't know about you, but I'm starving. Tokyo has so many amazing places to eat—choosing is the hardest part!

What are **YOU** having for dinner?

CHAPTER FOURTEEN

MIKA

"I DON'T GET IT." Mika stood in front of the mirror in the hotel bathroom, pinning her hair back with glittery blue barrettes. "I thought Chef Abe's restaurant was opening the night before the closing ceremony."

"It is," Dad said, straightening his tie. "This is the soft opening."

Mika wrinkled her nose. "What's the difference?"

"Well, for one thing, the soft opening isn't for the public," Dad told her. "It's not even advertised. Actually, Chef Abe probably won't serve his entire menu—we'll just be sampling some of his dishes."

"Is it like a dress rehearsal?"

"Exactly!" Dad's reflection beamed at her. "If it goes well, it can help generate buzz by word of mouth. Emi told me in confidence that several famous Olympic athletes were invited tonight. I think she's hoping they'll share photos and post on social media, so that by the real opening night, people will be lining up to get in!"

"Cool!" Mika gave him a bright smile, despite the fact that her stomach had been churning with nerves pretty much nonstop all day. In the morning, Mom had taken Mika and Andy to the official Olympic Games souvenir shop, where they'd bought T-shirts and hats and gifts for Devon, Riley, and Aunt Kei. Mika had found a little travel purse—white with a red dot like the Japanese flag—and showed it to Mom, fully expecting her to tell Mika she didn't need a purse. But to her surprise, Mom just smiled.

"I can get it? Really?" Mika asked excitedly.

"Absolutely," Mom replied. "Dad and I talked about it, and while we're sorry we're both very busy with work on this trip, we're proud of you and Andy for being so responsible."

That was when Mika's excitement had turned into guilt. She'd managed to hide her worries from Mom, but Andy obviously knew something was going on. Mika desperately wanted to tell him about A_Fan. She'd gotten another direct message from the account right after Team SuperFan found the Silver medal. *Ouch, so close again. That's gotta hurt.* Mika had looked around wildly, trying to spot anyone lurking nearby, but the viewing area for the giant clock had been filled with people.

She hadn't seen Gavin Driscoll the previous day, but he could've been there. Despite what Andy had said, Mika thought her theory that Gavin just might be trying to spice up his documentary on *OlympiFan* made sense. Plus, Gavin had been sitting behind Mika at the gymnastics event. She'd opened the photo in Instagram when he'd noticed it and complimented her; he could have seen that her handle was bluedreamphotos and looked it up later. Since Mika hadn't put a name or location on her profile, Gavin may have realized she was trying to keep her account a secret!

Mika had come so, so close to just telling Andy the entire story and showing him her Instagram account right then and there. But with three mysterious messages from someone who was clearly spying on her, Mika knew she shouldn't keep this a secret from her parents any longer. And if they found out Andy already knew about her Instagram account, he might get into trouble, too.

Besides, Mika was dreading telling all of them. If she had to do it, she'd rather tell them all at once. *Rip off the Band-Aid,* Riley would say. So Mika was going to rip off the Band-Aid tonight at dinner.

When the taxi pulled up to the same building where Dad had first met Chef Abe, Mom was waiting out front. She looked tired, but she smiled at Dad, Andy, and Mika as they climbed out of the taxi.

"Long day?" Dad asked, kissing her on the cheek.

"Very," Mom replied. "We covered the equestrian event, and I don't think I used enough sunscreen." She touched her cheek, and Mika noticed her face had a pink tinge. "Long day. But a fun day, too. What'd you guys do?"

As they entered the towering glass skyscraper and headed to the elevators, Andy told Mom all about the museum of technology that Dad had taken them to that afternoon. Mika stayed silent. She was so nervous that she was afraid if she opened her mouth, she'd just blurt out everything about Instagram, Enspire, and A_Fan right there in the elevator.

When the doors slid open, Mika stepped out first. "Ooh, look!"

They stepped off the elevator and into an expansive room with floor-to-ceiling windows. Outside, the sun was beginning to set, casting a bright glow onto the buildings that sprawled in all directions. The sky was rosy pink at the horizon, with layers of orange, purple, and deep midnight blue. At the center of the room was a circular island bar covered in mirrors, with 堅志, the kanji characters for the restaurant's name, written in enormous neon pink script behind the glass.

Mom whistled softly. "Snazzy place."

"I think it's going to be pretty spectacular," Dad said eagerly.

"Tom!" Emi hurried over to greet them, wearing a wrap dress the exact same shade of red as her glasses. Her graying hair was swept up with a gold comb that shone under the lights. "So good to see you. Andy and Mika, welcome. And you must be Karen!"

Mom held out her hand, and Emi shook it firmly. "It's wonderful to meet you," Mom said. "Thank you so much for inviting us."

"Of course, of course!" Emi led them past the expansive dining room and down a hallway.

Mika cast a longing look back at all the windows. "We're not eating in there?"

"Not tonight!" Emi said cheerfully. "This is a much more intimate gathering, and there's still a little bit of construction work left to do on the bar. We'll be dining in what's going to be Kenji's private room. I think you'll like it," she added with a big smile.

They followed her to a second elevator, which led to a small foyer with a chandelier made of sparkling purple crystals hanging overhead. Emi pushed open a door made of tinted glass and gestured for them to enter first. Mika stepped inside and blinked; the room was dimly lit, and it took a moment for her eyes to adjust. Her mouth fell open.

A long banquet table stretched out in front of her, perfectly centered in the rectangular room. Most of the chairs were already filled, and a low buzz of conversation was just audible over the soft string music that seemed to be coming from walls that looked like they were made out of bronze mesh. The only light came from strips lining the floorboards, like the tiny bulbs illuminating the aisles in a theater.

But the best part of the private room had to be the ceiling. Or rather, the lack of a ceiling. It took Mika a moment to realize it was a skylight, and not just open air. Thanks to the room's dim light, there was barely any reflection obscuring the view. All she could see overhead was the night sky, deep blue with twinkling stars that were just beginning to emerge.

"My goodness," Mom breathed, gazing up. "This is certainly something."

"Glad you like it." Emi showed them to their seats, which were at the opposite end of the room. As they walked past the long table, Mika tried to sneak a peek at the other guests without being too obvious. Dad had said there would be Olympic athletes in attendance, and she spotted Wesley and Hana right away. She recognized a few others too, including a young woman with short-cropped, blonde hair. The woman caught Mika's eye and smiled. Mika felt her face flush as she returned the smile before scurrying to her chair.

"That's Linda McDouglas!" she whispered to Andy, trying to point without being too obvious. "I recognize her from that Enspire commercial!"

"Who?" Andy asked as he sat down. Mika took the seat next to him, hanging her new purse over the back of the chair.

"Linda McDouglas. She's a Paralympic swimmer. Her right foot was amputated after an accident when she was little." Mika pulled out her phone and did a quick search. "Linda's won *eight* Paralympic medals!" she said in awe.

"Awesome." Andy took Mika's phone to read the rest of Linda's bio. To Mika's right, an older man with what looked like a permanent scowl sat taking notes in a small, black journal. His handwriting was impossibly tiny and neat. When he caught Mika staring, his scowl deepened, and he moved his arm to hide his writing.

Embarrassed, Mika turned away just as a busboy appeared carrying a tray of drinks. His hair was cut in a long fringe that hung almost down to his eyes, and while she couldn't quite place it, there was something about the expression on his face that felt vaguely familiar. He set a glass filled with ice, cherries, and something fizzy and pink in front of her before moving on to Andy. Mika took a sip and looked around, noticing that she and Andy were the only ones with this drink. All of the other guests were adults, and most of them had wine or tea.

"This place is so fancy," Mika whispered to Andy. When he didn't respond, she nudged him with her elbow. "Andy?"

"Sorry!" Andy didn't take his eyes off her screen. "Listen to this. Linda McDouglas says when she was in high school, her two passions were swim team and coding club. And there's a quote! 'I always thought coding would lead to a career, and swimming would be for fun. But it turned out to be the other way around!'"

Andy gave Mika a meaningful look. After a few seconds, she realized what he was thinking.

"You think she's the Masked Medalist?"

"I think she should be on our list, at least!" Andy handed her phone back, and Mika slipped it into her purse. "We've got to find the Gold. We really need those hints."

"I know." Mika watched Linda McDouglas for a few more seconds, then looked around the table. "I think almost everyone here is famous."

Andy nodded. "See that guy wearing a bow tie? I'm pretty sure I saw him on a movie poster in the subway station yesterday."

Following his gaze, Mika spotted the young man with the stylized messy hair and the silver bow tie at the other end of the table.

"Yeah, I recognize him, too!" Mika couldn't wait to tell Riley about this. "Even the busboy looked familiar. Did you notice?"

"Yeah," Andy said, nodding. "I think I *did* see him on the bus, now that you mention it . . ."

Mika poked his arm. "Ha ha, very funny. Not."

"Well, I thought it was funny. Hey, did you see this?"

Andy pointed to a small menu to the left of Mika's plate. She narrowed her eyes in the dim light to see a list of courses in both Japanese and English.

"Twelve courses?" she said, trying to keep her voice low. "Holy cow, that's a lot."

"I know, it's—" Andy stopped, pulling out his phone. Mika could see the text from Devon on his screen.

> **DP:** New post! Same message as the update, but the pic is cool.

Beneath the message was a link to the Masked Medalist's Instagram. Mika moved closer as Andy opened it. Her eyes widened when she saw the photo—a unique building that looked like a Rubik's Cube with each floor twisted just slightly out of line with the one below it.

"That building!" Mika whispered. "Didn't we pass that on our way here? It's really close! And look—they just posted this like fifteen minutes ago!"

"Whoa, I think you're right!"

Mika could tell Andy was thinking the same thing she was. They were at a fancy dinner with lots of Olympic athletes.

Maybe the Masked Medalist really was one of them!

She stared around at the table with renewed interest, while Andy leaned across the table to get Mom's attention. "Do you know all of the athletes here?" he asked, and Mom set down her glass and looked around.

"Let's see . . . well, you both know Hana and Wesley, obviously. Then there's Linda McDouglas and Gustav Binet, both Paralympic athletes." Mom leaned across Dad to see farther down the table. "I believe that's Paola Mazzanti, the cyclist—her nickname is Signorina Butterfly because of that birthmark on her neck! And then Chiang Li, on the other side of Emi . . ."

"Chiang Li?" Andy interrupted, craning his neck to look at the man chatting to Emi.

Mom nodded. "Table tennis. He's phenomenal."

Mika elbowed Andy again. "What?"

"Gavin Driscoll mentioned him, remember?" Andy whispered. "At the gymnastics event, when I asked if he had any idea who the Masked Medalist was. He said a lot of players think it's Chiang because he has a bunch of programming degrees."

"Oh yeah!"

Mika fell silent as Emi stood at the head of the table and cleared her throat.

"*Kenjiresutoran e yokoso.* Welcome to Kenji Restaurant," she began. Mika listened as Emi continued in Japanese, occasionally catching a word she knew, like *oishii*, which meant "*delicious.*" Her mind wandered back to A_Fan, and she winced. Now that she was here, she couldn't imagine telling her parents about her Instagram account during dinner, surrounded by famous athletes and actors. *Or maybe,* Mika told herself, *they won't get as mad with all of these people around.* She pressed a hand to her belly, which was rumbling—partly from hunger, partly from uneasiness.

Andy gave her a strange look. "Are you okay?" he whispered, and Mika nodded.

Once Emi had taken her seat, the waiters reappeared. Mika nudged Andy as a waiter placed tiny plates in front of them, each with a bundle of long white enoki mushrooms wrapped in bacon and drizzled with a deep-red sauce. The busboy reappeared to refill their water. His eyes briefly met Mika's before he moved on to the older man. Mika continued watching him, but he wouldn't make eye contact again. Still, she had the strangest sense that he'd recognized her, too.

"Where've we seen him before?" she asked Andy, who'd already eaten half of his mushroom bundle.

He shrugged. "Dunno. These bacon mushroom thingies are so good, but do you think all of the courses are going to be this small?"

Mika giggled, taking a bite of her appetizer. It was delicious—warm and savory, and the bacon was extra crispy. Her appetite returned with a vengeance. She polished it off quickly and wiped her mouth on her napkin. *No revealing secrets at dinner,* she decided. *I'll do it as soon as we get back to the hotel.*

The next three courses were just as delicious as the first—and just as small. But the fourth course—a salmon soufflé with truffle sauce, according to the menu—wasn't so little. Each course after that seemed to increase in size, and by the time she'd finished the ninth course (wagyu beef served in individual miniskillets), Mika was too full of delicious food to bother thinking about A_Fan.

"I'm stuffed," Andy announced, setting down his fork. Across the table, Mom laughed.

"Three courses to go!" she said. "But I believe they're all dessert."

Mika perked up. "Ooh . . . I definitely have room for that."

She felt someone brush against the back of her chair and jumped, startled, as the busboy removed the skillet from her place. "Thank you," she said, trying to get a better look at his face, but he nodded and hurried off quickly. *Where* had she seen him before?

Three black sesame cookies, two chocolate-covered strawberries, and one cup of herbal tea later, Mika felt ready to burst. Chef Abe suddenly appeared at the other end of the table, and everyone applauded—even the older man next to Mika grudgingly joined in. Hana cupped her hands around her mouth and released a piercing whistle that caused Wesley to cover his ears while everyone laughed and Chef Abe blushed. Mika expected the young chef to say something, but he just gave a shy smile and a quick nod before disappearing.

"If that was a dress rehearsal, I think opening night is gonna be amazing," she told Dad as they stood to go, slinging her purse over her shoulder.

Dad laughed. "I think you might be right about that."

"Aw, did Chiang Li already leave?" Andy stood on tiptoe, looking down the table.

Mika giggled. "What were you going to do, walk up to him and say, 'Hey, are you the Masked Medalist?' "

"Maybe!" Andy said, then sighed. "Okay, no."

When they stepped off the elevator, Mom yawned hugely, covering her mouth with her hand. "Between spending all day out in the sun and that incredible meal, I'm going to sleep like a baby tonight."

"Me too," Mika agreed. But now that they were heading back to the hotel, her nerves had returned. Was it too late to have a big talk with her parents? It might be inconsiderate, given that Mom was so tired. Maybe Mika should just put the whole Band-Aid-ripping thing off until morning.

They'd nearly exited the building when she reached into her purse for her phone—and froze.

"Uh-oh."

"What's wrong?" Dad asked.

Mika rummaged around in her purse, then pulled it open wide and stared. "My phone's gone!"

"You left it in the restaurant?"

"No, I . . ." Mika paused, frowning. "I took it out to show Andy something, but I definitely put it back in my purse. I didn't take it out after that."

"Are you sure?" Andy asked.

"Yes! I wanted to take pictures of the food, but it was so dark, I figured they wouldn't come out."

Dad pushed his glasses up his nose. "Okay. Let's go back and take a look."

Mom and Andy waited in the lobby while Dad and Mika walked back to the elevators. Mika went over and over the evening in her mind, trying to think of what she could have done with her phone.

A few of Chef Abe's guests still lingered around the table in the private dining room, chatting, as Mika hurried over to her chair. She spotted the older journalist who had been sitting next to her, now deep in conversation with Hana at the other end of the table. Hana caught Mika's eye and gave her a little wave as the journalist continued talking, and Mika waved back.

Paola Mazzanti was now seated in the journalist's chair, chatting with the actor in the bow tie. Mika scooted past them and noticed the birthmark Mom had mentioned—it really was shaped exactly like a butterfly!

Feeling extremely self-conscious, Mika dropped to her knees to check under her chair. There was no sign of her phone. *Was* it at the hotel? It was so unlike Mika to lose something important like this . . .

"*Scusami?* Did you lose something?"

Blushing, Mika looked up to see Paola watching her in concern. "Oh! Yes, my phone."

Paola's face brightened. "Ah! What color?"

"Um, blue? With hearts on it?"

With a flourish, Paola picked up a phone on the other side of her teacup.

Relief flooded through Mika when she recognized

the blue case. "That's it! Where did you find it?"

"Right here," Paola responded, still smiling. "Hiding under a napkin. I was going to give it to Emi if no one returned to claim it."

"Thank you so much," Mika said fervently, slipping her phone in her purse. "Have a good night!"

Her relief was quickly replaced by confusion. The journalist had still been sitting there when Mika and her family had left. So how had her phone ended up in his spot?

"Found it," she told Dad, who smiled.

"Great!"

They took the elevators back down and hurried across the lobby, Mika still trying to figure out what had happened. Maybe the journalist had spotted her phone on the floor after she'd gone . . . but why would he leave it under his napkin instead of giving it to Emi? For that matter, how had Mika's phone fallen out of her purse, when it had been hanging on her chair all evening?

She and Andy followed their parents down the block, where Dad said it would be easier to catch a taxi. At the intersection, the street was lit up with neon signs and digital billboards in all four directions. Mika stared absentmindedly at the billboard directly across the street advertising an upcoming anime convention. Suddenly the screen changed . . . and the Enspire logo appeared.

Mika found herself staring at her own photo!

It was her first post, the two little girls at the gymnastics event, with bluedreamphotos and *#TeamWorld* emblazoned at the bottom of the screen. The whole thing was so huge and epic and unreal that it didn't even register at first. Then Mika felt a huge grin stretching across her cheeks, and she clapped both hands over her mouth.

Enspire had used her photo!

Her photo! It was right there, on a gigantic flashy billboard right in the middle of Tokyo! Mika's brain felt jammed. She had to text Riley. No—first she had to take a picture! A picture of her picture! A wild giggle escaped her throat as she fumbled for her phone, swiping on the camera . . .

And then she saw Dad and Andy staring at the billboard, too.

Andy figured it out first. He turned to gape at Mika, who froze. Dad had stepped onto the curb to flag a taxi, but his arm dropped as he turned to face Mika, too. His eyebrows were raised, and his mouth was in a grim line.

Mom looked around at them questioningly. "What's going on?"

Mika swallowed hard, but she said nothing. Dad cleared his throat, giving Mom a pointed look.

"I think Mika has something to tell us."

OLYMPIFAN UPDATE!

Locations for the Gold Medal

Hello again, OlympiFans!
Hard to believe we're nearing the end of the
Games—and the end of **OUR** game, too. I've received
tons of messages asking if teams can take a guess at
my identity before all the medals are found.
The answer is: yes!

But!

Be warned that each team gets only **ONE** guess.
If you guess wrong, that's it!
So go find that Gold and get those hints!
Here are the locations where the final
clues are waiting . . .

Akasaka
Roppongi/Azabu
Imperial Palace Area
Hibiya Park
Nishi-Shinbashi

Happy clue hunting, OlympiFans!

CHAPTER FIFTEEN

ANDY

WHEN ANDY WOKE up the next morning, his first thought was about exploring the locations for the clues to the Gold medal.

His second thought was that it didn't matter, because he couldn't play *OlympiFan* anymore.

Mom and Dad hadn't grounded Mika—not yet, anyway. They hadn't done *anything*. They'd listened as she explained in a shaky voice that she had created an anonymous Instagram account to enter the Enspire contest. Neither of them looked angry, but Andy knew from experience that those calm, neutral expressions meant something even worse than anger: Mom and Dad were disappointed.

The taxi ride back to the hotel had been completely silent. The only time his parents had spoken was when Mom told them to get ready for bed, and Dad had added that they should plan on spending the morning at the hotel while he worked. Although Andy and Mika had been able to hear them talking on the other side of the door for some time, their parents' voices had been too soft for them to really overhear anything.

Andy could tell that waiting for the verdict was probably a worse punishment for Mika than actually being grounded. She'd sat up in bed for hours, her phone untouched on her nightstand, staring blankly at the muted movie on their television. A part of Andy felt bad for his sister; he'd been tempted to crack a joke or do something to make her laugh and relax a little. He'd also wanted to tell her that it had been incredibly awesome to see her photo on that giant billboard in the middle of the city—because it really had been *awesome*.

But he didn't say any of that. Because another, bigger, slightly bitter part of Andy was hurt that she hadn't told him her secret. Had she thought he would tell Mom and Dad? It wasn't like she'd joined Instagram because Riley had, or to post selfies and pictures from their trip. In Andy's opinion, she'd actually had a good reason for breaking their parents' rule. He'd looked at the other pictures she'd posted, and it was obvious that Mika had talent. Her photos were really good. Better than really good. They were *great*. And he would have told her so, if she'd bothered to trust him enough to show him what she was doing.

And then there was *OlympiFan*. Andy couldn't help but be upset that Mika had pretty much ruined their ability to play in AR mode. Obviously Mom and Dad weren't going to let her explore Tokyo unchaperoned now. And if Mika couldn't be out of her parents' sight, then neither could Andy. With both Mom and Dad busy working, Andy and Mika were going to be stuck at the hotel . . . a lot.

So when Mika finally crawled out of bed, rubbing her eyes sleepily, Andy didn't say anything. Neither did she. The silence expanded like a balloon all morning, until by the time they'd finished breakfast and Dad had returned to the hotel's business center to work, the air felt thick and tense, like at any moment, there might be a *pop!*

Andy decided to stay in the lobby, figuring it might be slightly less boring than their hotel room. He plopped down on one of the long gray sofas and opened *Olympi-Fan*. A moment later, Mika sat on one of the plush armchairs across from him. He ignored her and began to play in VR mode, choosing Hibiya Park as his first location. A fun fact popped up almost immediately:

Did you know this park is home to a 500-year-old ginkgo tree?

Andy sighed, irritated. Right now, he and Mika could be walking around this park for real if she hadn't gotten in trouble. VR mode was fine, but Andy had enjoyed exploring Tokyo in real life.

More importantly, there was only one medal left. If Team MADR didn't find the Gold, they wouldn't have a chance at winning the grand prize. Andy thought about Chiang Li and Linda McDouglas and all the other athletes at dinner last night. Without the hints, his chances of guessing the Masked Medalist's identity were next to nothing. Andy just *had* to figure out where the Gold medal was first.

It didn't take long before he found the first clue: the number 487. The next clue was 52, and the third was 112. When he checked his team's clue collection page, he saw the app had stacked them vertically, with the lowest number on the bottom:

487
112
52

Andy couldn't help but grin. Numbers were definitely a universal language, and he felt pretty confident in his fluency. Math was his favorite subject at school, and he loved number puzzles like cryptograms and sudoku.

"What are you smiling at?"

The sound of Mika's voice after all the tense silence was startling. Andy glanced at her and felt bad about how nervous she looked.

"The clues for the Gold are numbers," he explained.

"Ah." Mika tried to smile, but Andy caught the guilt flashing across her face. And just like that, any anger he had toward her vanished. However bad Andy felt about their situation, it was nothing compared to what Mika was going through. After all, she was the one who'd gotten in trouble.

"Are you going to play?" he asked, noticing for the first time that Mika didn't have her phone out. In fact, he hadn't seen it all morning. Had Mom and Dad taken it away earlier without him noticing? Andy had been surprised that they hadn't immediately deleted Instagram from her phone. He couldn't help but wonder if Mom and Dad were secretly proud of Mika's photo being featured by the Enspire campaign, too.

After a moment's hesitation, Mika reached into her backpack and pulled out her phone.

"I do want to play," she said, casting Andy an uncertain look. "But first, there's something I need to show you."

"Okay . . ." Andy watched curiously as Mika swiped her screen, then held her phone out. Instagram was open, but he wasn't looking at pictures or posts, just a series of messages:

> **A_Fan:** Do your parents know what a talented photographer their daughter is?

> **A_Fan:** No luck with the pandas? Too bad.

> **A_Fan:** Ouch, so close again. That's gotta hurt.

> **A_Fan:** Clues for the Gold are up. Or are you just going to steal those hints, too?

Andy blinked. "What is this?"

"Direct messages. I tried going to that account to see who it is, but they don't have any posts or followers. I think whoever it is made that account just to send me messages. My name isn't anywhere on my account, Andy. I was so careful to keep it a secret, but I guess someone figured out it was me!"

The words all came out in a rush, and Andy was startled to see Mika's eyes fill with tears. He looked back down at the screen and felt a small seed of anger bloom deep in his gut.

"The pandas," he said slowly, and Mika nodded.

"Yeah, they sent that message when we were *at the zoo!*" she cried. "A_Fan knew I was there, *and* they knew about the note. And the next one was sent right when that other team won the Silver—like they knew I was there, too. They knew how close we came to winning. I think . . . I think A_Fan's following me."

Fear began to mingle with the anger now rapidly coursing through Andy's veins. Was someone trying to scare his sister? And *follow* her?

"Why didn't you tell Mom and Dad? Or *me*?" Andy demanded. "Seriously, why didn't you tell me about the whole Instagram thing? Did you think I'd tell on you or something?"

"No!" Fresh tears spilled down Mika's cheeks. "I thought if Mom and Dad found out and thought you knew, you'd get in trouble, too."

"But these messages . . ." Andy shook his head, scanning them again. "You got the first one last week. And this person mentioned the pandas—" Realization dawned, and Andy's mouth fell open. "This is the person who left us that note!"

Mika swallowed hard. "I think so, too. And . . . and I think maybe it's Gavin Driscoll."

Andy stared at his sister. "Why are you so sure it's him. Just because of that picture?"

"No, it's because . . ." Mika wiped her eyes and sniffled. "He was sitting behind us at the gymnastics event, remember? He complimented my photo. But the thing is, when he saw it, I had just opened Instagram. I hadn't posted the photo yet, but he definitely could've seen my handle. He's the only person I can think of besides Riley who knows!"

At the mention of Riley, Andy felt stung all over again. "Riley knows? Did you tell her about these messages, too?"

Mika shook her head emphatically. "I didn't tell anybody about those. Just you."

"Hey there, Kudo kids!"

Andy and Mika looked up, startled to see Valentina smiling down at them as she hugged a thick binder with the Compete logo to her chest. Behind her, Andy could see Mom and James walking into the lobby, followed by Hana and Wesley. Quickly, he tucked Mika's phone between the sofa cushions.

"Surprised you two aren't out adventuring," Valentina went on. "Too hot outside for you?"

Mika ducked her head, looking ashamed, and Andy answered quickly. "No, just thought we'd hang out here this morning. I thought Mom said she'd be at the broadcast center all day?"

"Change of plans," Valentina replied just as Mom joined them.

"Dad got called in to work," she explained. "Chef Abe is doing a photo shoot, and Emi wants Dad to write about it. He's up in the room getting ready. So we shuffled our schedule around and moved our meeting to the conference room here—much easier than getting you guys over to the broadcast center at the last minute."

At this, Mika looked guiltier than ever, even though Mom's tone was light. Andy thought that Mom looked like she might feel a little sorry for Mika, too.

"After this meeting, how about I take you both out for lunch?" Mom said, placing a hand on Mika's shoulder. "You guys can pick the place."

"Okay!" Andy agreed, but Mika just nodded glumly. Mom patted her lightly on the back before heading to the conference room with Valentina and James.

Hana and Wesley trailed behind, deep in conversation. As they passed the sofa, Andy overheard Wesley say, "Emi said they searched the whole private room. No sign of it."

"Are you sure you didn't leave it charging at the broadcast center?" Hana asked dryly. "You've done that before." She caught Andy staring and winked at him. "Wesley lost his phone . . . again."

"Andy does that all the time!" Mika blurted out. "We almost missed our plane coming here because he left it charging at home."

"You're the one who lost your phone last night," Andy shot back as Wesley turned to Mika.

"Wait—at the restaurant?"

"Yeah! I found it, though," Mika said.

Wesley sighed. "Well, mine's just *gone*. And yes, I'm one-hundred-percent positive I didn't leave it at the broadcast center," he added, giving Hana a mock-angry look.

"We'll see when we check the lost and found," Hana said sweetly, and Mika giggled. "See you two later!"

"Bye!"

Once the conference room doors had closed, Andy pulled Mika's phone out from between the cushions. Remembering those messages from A_Fan made his stomach drop.

"Are you absolutely positive that nobody but Gavin knows about your Instagram?" Andy asked.

Mika chewed her lip. "I don't know. He's the only person who saw it on my phone. How would anybody else find out?"

Andy drummed his fingers on the sofa cushion. This

was a puzzle, and he felt like he had most of the pieces already. He just had to put them into place.

Taking Mika's phone, Andy read A_Fan's messages again. "*Clues for the Gold are up,*" he said aloud. "*Or are you just going to steal those hints, too?*"

"Yeah, what does that even mean?" Mika exclaimed. "Do they think that somehow I stole the hints that came with the other medals? I mean, how would someone even *do* that?"

Andy gazed at her, his mind working overtime. "Someone could hack into a player's account."

"What?"

"Someone might have hacked into the accounts of the players on the winning teams and seen the hints." Andy's spine tingled as he felt the pieces shift into place. "So A_Fan must be on one of the winning teams. Didn't A_Fan start messaging you after TilerMyths won the Bronze?"

"Yeah, but that was on my Instagram account." Mika wrinkled her nose. "And then there was that message about visiting the zoo. But how is it connected? Why would A_Fan think I saw the hints TilerMyths won? How would they even know?"

"They wouldn't," Andy said. "Unless . . ."

Mika's confusion only lasted a moment. Then her eyes went wide. "*Oh.* You don't think . . ."

Andy nodded. "I do. I think A_Fan *is* TilerMyths."

SCOREBOARD - TOP TEN

1st	⭐	SuperFan	1,057
2nd	⭐	Cryptic	602
3rd	⭐	TamborAoSol	478
4th		베스트	466
5th		MysticMice	452
6th		XYZGirls	449
7th		ALLEYOOP	447
8th		CyFyBorgs	442
9th		Dragonflame	440
10th		MADR	439

CHAPTER SIXTEEN

MIKA

CONFUSED, MIKA WATCHED as Andy pulled out his phone and opened *OlympiFan.*

"What are you doing?" she asked.

"From these messages, it sounds like someone hacked into TilerMyths' account to see the hints, and he thinks it was you. So then he left that note with the clue at the shrine . . . oh, wait." Andy slumped back in the sofa. "Whoever left that note did it right after Tiler found the Bronze. There wouldn't have been enough time for him to realize his account had been hacked *and* write that note."

Mika could tell Andy was frustrated. "Do you think TilerMyths might be Gavin?" she asked in a small voice. "He's making that documentary, and he was at the Meiji Shrine. And my photo . . ."

"He's friends with Dad," Andy said, shaking his head. "I really don't think Gavin's playing *OlympiFan*, Mika. He's always watching events, or filming stuff. He's not sitting around playing a game on his phone every time we see him. And TilerMyths is *good.* He's always in the top ten on the scoreboard."

"They," Mika corrected automatically. "Team Cryptic is at the top of the scoreboard. TilerMyths has a teammate, even if that player isn't as good as he is."

Andy stared at her. "You're right. That player might not be as good at collecting clues, but maybe they left the note!"

Quickly, he opened Team Cryptic's page, and Mika leaned over to see the screen. Like TilerMyths, the other player's profile was mostly blank. Their player name was UppeRcase.

"It's a cryptogram!" Andy exclaimed, sitting up straight.

Mika frowned. "What?"

Andy looked excited. "Look—the word itself is a clue to decipher it. *UppeRcase.* The *U* and the *R* are uppercase letters, and the rest are lowercase. Do you have a pencil?"

"Yeah." Mika dug one from her backpack and handed it to Andy. He grabbed a notepad off the table next to the sofa and wrote:

Uppe//Rcase

"It's two words," he explained. "Maybe it's the person's

first and last name! They could've used a cipher alphabet to code it. I might be able to figure it out if I start with the vowels . . ."

Mika watched as Andy started to scribble. Her mind wandered back to finding the note at the Meiji Shrine. She had to admit, what Andy said about Gavin made sense. Someone else had probably left the note. Mika closed her eyes, trying to remember exactly what happened after Andy almost won the Bronze. He'd been on the side of the path, looking at *OlympiFan*. But Mika's mind had been on her first Instagram post. So she'd opened it up, scrolled through the likes, seen one from Enspire, and then . . .

"Oh."

Andy didn't glance up from his work. "'Oh,' what?"

Dread filled Mika as she pointed at his notepad. "Try *e* for *u* and *a* for *e*."

"Okay . . ." Andy obliged, then showed her the paper.

$$E\_\_a\;//\;\_\_\_\_a$$

Mika stifled a groan. "*M* for *p*."

Andy started to write again, then looked up at her sharply. "*Emma?*"

"Emma Botha." Mika felt dazed. "She got to the shrine right after us—right after TilerMyths found the Bronze. I was looking at my Instagram when she came up to me . . . she could've seen my handle. I bet she did." Her confusion began to fade, replaced with anger. "And then she asked me to take a photo of her under the gate, standing *in the exact spot where I found the note.* After she left, I wanted to take the same photo, so I asked you. Remember? And that's when I found the note!"

Grimacing, she opened her messages.

Andy leaned forward. "What are you doing?"

"Texting her."

"Mika, *wait—*"

But Mika had already sent the text.

> **MK:** Hi!! Wanna meet up later, look for OlympiFan clues? 🔍

Andy read the message, then gave her a pointed look. "We can't actually meet up with her. No going anywhere without Mom and Dad anymore, remember?"

He didn't say it accusingly, but Mika winced anyway. For a few glorious minutes, she'd managed to forget all about the trouble she was in with her parents.

"Right. Um." Mika stared down at her phone, feeling deflated. "What do I do? Text again and say *never mind?*"

"Tell her you can't because you're grounded and you forgot," Andy said with a perfectly straight face.

"First of all, no. Second of all, I'm not *technically* grounded. Mom and Dad never used that word."

"You will be, though."

"I know." Mika slumped back into the armchair, making a face at her phone. "Maybe it won't matter. Maybe she won't text me back." But even as she spoke, the bubbles popped up on the left side of her screen. Mika sat up straight. "Oh wait! She's typing!" She got up and sat on the sofa next to Andy so he could read Emma's response.

EB: Sure! Can u meet me? I'm at the Continental Hotel Akasaka. Lots of clues here!! 🔍

"The Continental Hotel Akasaka," Andy said quietly. "She did leave that note—remember the hotel logo on the other side of the paper?"

Mika read the text five times, struggling with a strange mix of emotions. Emma seemed so nice, like she really wanted to be Mika's friend. But those Instagram messages had really frightened Mika. And why in the world did Emma think Mika had stolen her team's hints?

"We need to talk to her and explain we didn't steal anything." Mika chewed her lip, thinking. Then she started typing again.

"What are you going to say?" Andy asked, trying to see her screen. "We can't go anywhere, remember?"

"Don't worry," Mika said as she sent the text. "I have an idea."

TEAM ALLEYOOP CHAT ROOM

Shellbee: Update???

Beeyanca: Ugh

Shellbee: Uh oh. He wasn't at the hedgehog café?

Feebee: He was. We got his autograph!

Shellbee: OMG you actually TALKED to Zahir Long?!?!?!

Feebee: Yeah!! But he's not the Masked Medalist.

Shellbee: Aw. Are you sure? I mean, of course he'd say no if you just asked him outright. I told you guys, that's kind of like cheating. (Sorry, B.)

Feebee: I know. But I'm pretty sure he wasn't lying. Back to square one.

Beeyanca: UGH

TEAM SUPERFAN CHAT ROOM

IronMatt: Running late! Be there in 15!

AgentAngel: It's ok. Still waiting for SuperZuki and SabineTheGreat.

AgentAngel: We're at the Otemon entrance btw.

IronMatt: 👍

SabineTheGreat: Almost there. SuperZuki isn't coming.

AgentAngel: Oh no! Why?

SabineTheGreat: Long story. Think we lost a teammate. ☹

TEAM DRAGONFLAME CHAT ROOM

MageMisaki: I seriously want to report whoever left that note at the shrine and get them banned from the game.

CentaurCici: Told you it wasn't a real clue. 📷

CHAPTER SEVENTEEN

ANDY

BY THE TIME Mom emerged from the conference room almost an hour later, Mika and Andy had agreed on a plan. "We still haven't had ramen yet," Mika said, wearing her most innocent expression. "I looked up a few ramen shops and there's a really good one in Akasaka close to the stadium. Can we go there?"

"Sounds perfect!" Mom agreed, and Andy breathed a sigh of relief. He gave Mika a thumbs-up and they followed Mom outside to hail a taxi. As they all stepped out to the curb, Andy watched Mika type a response to Emma.

> **MK:** We're having lunch at the ramen shop near your hotel! Meet us there?

No sooner had Andy climbed into the taxi and buckled his seat belt than Mika showed him her phone again.

> **EB:** Ok! ☺👌

Andy grimaced. Just like with Gavin, this didn't feel exactly right. Emma seemed really nice. Was she trying to hide the fact that she was on Team Cryptic? It *was* hard to imagine her sending those direct messages to Mika.

"Everything okay?" Mom asked, twisting around in the front seat to look at them. When Mika hastily shoved her phone in her pocket, Mom arched an eyebrow. "Anything you want to tell me?"

Mika's cheeks blazed red. "Well . . ."

"Remember Emma?" Andy interrupted. "The girl Mika and I sat with at the track-and-field event?" When Mom nodded, he continued. "She texted Mika to see if we wanted to hang out, and we know her hotel is close to this ramen place, so we asked her to come."

Andy didn't add that this was the whole reason they'd picked the ramen shop in the first place. He suspected Mom guessed as much, anyway, because she looked slightly amused.

"What a coincidence!" She turned to look at Mika, who slumped down in her seat. "Look, honey. I know we still need to have a talk about what you did. You broke a pretty important rule, and Dad and I are still discussing what we're going to do about it. But we both agree on one thing."

Andy glanced at Mika, who sat completely still, not even blinking as she waited for Mom to finish.

"Being here in Tokyo during the Olympics is a once-in-a-lifetime opportunity, and making you stay at a hotel and miss all the excitement isn't a fair punishment." Mom paused, glancing at Andy. "And it'd be especially unfair to your brother, because we're not about to let either one of you wander around the city alone. So while we're here, you won't be grounded. And you don't need to make up ways to meet up with your friends or play *OlympiFan*. Our trip rules haven't changed."

Mika's shoulders slumped as she let out a sigh, and Andy saw Mom's lips quirk up.

"But we *will* have a discussion about this Instagram thing as soon as the trip is over. And there will be consequences for your actions. Understood?"

"Yes." Mika nodded vigorously. "Thanks, Mom."

As soon as Mom turned around in her seat, Andy and Mika exchanged grins. Andy felt a surge of relief. He wouldn't be stuck at the hotel for the rest of the trip! He could keep playing *OlympiFan* in AR mode. Maybe their team still had a shot at finding that Gold medal and figuring out the Masked Medalist's identity.

But first, they had to have a talk with Emma.

Andy lifted a huge pile of steaming ramen noodles and pork between his chopsticks. The flavorful broth, combined with his nerves over confronting Emma, had him feeling almost feverishly warm in the little shop. He was grateful for the air conditioning unit over the window blasting frigid air onto their table.

Across from him, Mom laughed as Andy tried in vain to slurp all of his noodles down at once.

"Sorry," Andy said once he'd finally managed to swallow. "I didn't mean to be so noisy."

"Actually, slurping your noodles is considered polite in Japan," Mom said, picking up her own noodles with her chopsticks. "It lets the chef know you find the food delicious."

"Really?" Andy glanced at his sister and grinned. "Then Mika's *extra* polite."

Mika ignored him, her cheeks bulging like a chipmunk's as she slurped more noodles from her bowl.

After draining the last bit of broth, Mom glanced at her watch. "I hope your friend gets here soon!" she said. "I'd like a chance to say hi before I leave."

Mika paused with another enormous bite of noodles halfway to her mouth, her gaze fixed on the entrance. "There she is!"

Andy swiveled on his stool just as Emma spotted them. She smiled and waved, and he tried to smile back. But inside, he was nervous—and a little bit angry, too. Emma seemed so friendly, but she had really freaked Mika out with those Instagram messages.

"Hello," Mom said cheerfully when Emma approached the table. "We didn't get a chance to meet at the race the other day."

"Hi, Mrs. Kudo! Nice to meet you," Emma said politely. Her gaze flicked to the menu hanging over the counter, and her eyes lit up. "Ooh, they have mochi ice cream! You guys want some?"

"I'm afraid I have to get to work." Mom was already standing and slinging her laptop bag over her shoulder. "But I'm sure these two would love some!"

"I'll be right back!" Emma hurried off, and Mom turned to Andy and Mika.

"Have fun, and remember the rules," she said. "I'll see you at the stadium in . . . ?"

"Two hours," Andy and Mika chorused. Mom gave them both a quick hug before heading out of the shop.

Exhaling, Andy glanced at his sister. She'd set her chopsticks down, that last bite of noodles uneaten. If Mika was leaving food in her bowl, she must be *really* nervous.

Emma reappeared holding a plate piled with little balls in pastel colors. "You guys have had these before, right?"

"Yeah, lots of times." Andy plucked a strawberry mochi ice cream off the plate and took a bite. The soft, sticky rice cakes filled with ice cream were one of his favorite treats from Dough Re Mi, a bakery across the street from his school back in Los Angeles.

"So, where'd you guys want to start looking for clues?" Emma asked, selecting a chocolate one. She paused, glancing from Mika to Andy, and her expression changed. "What's up?"

Andy set down the rest of his mochi. "We know you left that note about the pandas," he said, at the exact same time as Mika blurted out: "Why'd you send me all of those messages on Instagram?"

Emma bit her lip but didn't say anything. Calmly, she finished her dessert and wiped her fingers on a napkin.

Andy felt a flash of impatience. "Well? You *are* on Team Cryptic, right?"

"Yeah," Emma said, clasping her hands on the table. "But—"

"And you left that note at the Meiji Shrine?"

"Yes, but—"

"And you knew about my Instagram account!" Mika interrupted. "And you created that A_Fan account just to send me weird messages!"

Emma gaped. "What are you talking about?"

"Come on," Mika said, leaning forward. "My Instagram account was a secret. You saw it when we met at the shrine, didn't you? You saw my handle and you looked it up."

"Yeah, I saw it," Emma admitted. "Bluedreamphotos. Your pictures are really good. But what weird messages are you talking about?"

Looking exasperated, Mika pulled out her phone. After a few seconds of swiping, she held it out to Emma. Andy could see the messages from A_Fan on the screen, and he watched Emma's reaction carefully. She looked completely confused.

"That's not me," she said. "I swear. I'm on Instagram, and I did follow you, but that's not my account!"

"Yeah, right," Mika muttered. "Who else could it be?"

"I don't . . ." Emma paused, her eyes darting down to her own phone. Then she groaned. "Oh, no."

"What?" Andy asked.

Sighing, Emma looked from him to Mika. "I bet that's Tyler."

"Tyler?" Andy repeated. "You mean *TilerMyths*? Your teammate?"

"Yeah." Emma pressed her lips together. "His name's Tyler Smith. He's a family friend—our moms are practically like sisters. We visited them a couple years ago. Tyler lives in New York, so he's been playing in VR mode."

Andy stared at her. TilerMyths . . . Tyler Smith. He'd used an anagram as his player name, just like Emma had used a cryptogram.

"I told him about meeting you guys, and about your Instagram, Mika." Emma's expression was defiant. "I only told him because I thought your photos were really cool. But when we looked at it and didn't see your name anywhere, we wondered if it was a secret account. You only had like two photos, and they both had #*TeamWorld*—like you'd just made the account to enter that contest."

Mika lifted her chin. "Yeah, that's exactly what I did. But these messages—you left that note, didn't you? The one about the pandas?"

"The notes were his idea," Emma began.

"Notes?" Andy interjected. "There was only one note!"

"You guys found one," Emma said. "But I left a few all around the Meiji Shrine. Fake clues."

"You were trying to cheat?" Mika asked in disbelief.

Emma's eyes flashed. "It's not cheating! It's just throwing players off the trail. *You* were trying to cheat."

"What?!"

"Anyone who found those notes and actually thought they were real clues had to know it'd be unfair to the other players," Emma said, crossing her arms. "That was part of Tyler's and my strategy. I wrote all the notes out ahead of time. Then, as soon as we figured out where the medal was, I got there as fast as I could to leave them lying around so other players who came close to winning would find them. We figured if a player found a note and ignored it, no harm done. But if they believed it . . . well, they deserved to get thrown off track a little. If you'd actually found the Silver medal at the zoo, what would you've done? Taken it, I bet. *That* would have been cheating."

Andy remembered how relieved he'd felt when he'd realized there was no medal at the panda exhibit. What *would* he have done if he'd found it? Because Emma was right—Andy had guessed that no other player had access to that clue. He knew there was no way the Masked Medalist had left that note. He knew it wasn't part of the game. But he'd still gone and looked for the Silver, just to be sure.

A blush had appeared on Mika's cheeks. "So what— you followed us to the zoo to see what we'd do?"

"She didn't have to follow us," Andy said suddenly. "I'm friends with Tyler on *OlympiFan*, so he could see my location."

"He was *spying* on us?" Mika said in disbelief.

"It's not *spying*," Emma said defensively. "It's just playing the game."

Andy couldn't help but agree. After all, he'd looked to see where all of the teams in the top ten were searching for clues countless times over the past several days.

"Okay, so the notes were part of your strategy," Andy said, reaching for his sister's phone. "But this direct message—*Clues for the Gold are up. Or are you just going to steal those hints, too?*" He stared at Emma. "Do you and Tyler seriously think we somehow stole your hints?"

Emma leaned back in her chair, tilting her head

back. "*Ugh,*" she groaned, and the sound was so similar to Mika's pitiful sheep bleating that Andy almost laughed. Straightening up, Emma took a deep breath. "I definitely do *not* think you guys did that," she said earnestly. "But someone did get into our account and see the hints. They left a message; it was so . . . uh, hang on."

Before Andy or Mika could respond, Emma picked up her phone and started tapping. A moment later, Andy heard ringing.

"Are you calling someone?"

"I'm FaceTiming Tyler," Emma said, leaning forward and stretching her arms across the table so that Andy and Mika could see the screen. "It's only midnight in New York, so I know he's still awake."

Sure enough, a second later the ringing stopped and a boy's face filled the screen. He had pale skin and wore wire-rimmed glasses and a Yankees baseball cap. "Emma?"

Emma gestured for Andy and Mika to lean in so that Tyler could see them. "Hey," she said shortly. "This is Andy and Mika Kudo. Have you been bothering her on Instagram?"

Tyler's eyes flared open briefly. Then he pulled a face. "Don't be so dramatic. I was just—"

"It's *wrong,* Tyler!" Emma yelled, and across the restaurant, a few heads turned in their direction. "Seriously, I *told* you they didn't hack our account. And even if they did, you can't just send a girl random messages like that! I can't believe you—"

"Okay, okay!" Tyler said, clearly exasperated. "I'm sorry, all right? I guess I was just angry that you weren't concentrating on playing the game and finding clues. It seemed like you were more interested in checking Instagram and hanging out with *her* than winning. But I'm sorry. I know I shouldn't have done it."

"Tell *her* that." Emma tilted the phone toward Mika, who looked as startled as a deer in headlights. "Well, go on!"

Andy watched as Tyler and Mika stared at one another. Finally, Mika cleared her throat.

"We didn't hack into your account," she said. "Honestly."

Slowly, Tyler's expression changed from exasperated to guilty.

"Okay. I'm sorry I sent those messages." He sounded like he meant it, and after a second, Mika nodded.

"Okay. Thanks."

Andy leaned forward. "But someone definitely hacked into your account?"

"Yup. Well, they hacked into Emma's account," Tyler corrected himself. "They left a message in our chat room saying they saw her leave the note at the Meiji Shrine, so they looked at the hints when we won the Bronze. You two were at the shrine, that's why I thought it was you."

"Yeah, but we didn't know Emma had left the note," Mika said. "We only just figured that out this morning!"

"And if we'd seen Emma leave the note, we wouldn't have looked for the medal at the zoo!" Andy pointed out. "We would've known it was fake."

Tyler frowned. "So you *were* going to cheat."

Andy opened his mouth to argue, but nothing came out. Once again, he tried to imagine what would have happened if the Silver medal had been in the panda exhibit. Would he really have just walked away and left it there?

"We are not cheaters," Mika told Tyler fiercely. "But someone out there is. So maybe stop leaving notes to throw people off and just play the game fairly."

"We *are* playing fair," Tyler retorted. "Those—"

"Maybe the notes were a bad idea," Emma interrupted, and Tyler groaned.

"It wasn't cheating, Emma, it was a strategy!"

"I know, but—"

"It's a pretty sneaky strategy," Andy said flatly. "But you're right—we fell for it, and if the Silver medal had been there, I might have taken it. But that's not the same as hacking into someone's account."

He stood up, and so did Mika. Emma looked worriedly back and forth between them. "Are you leaving?"

"We're going to look for clues," Andy said, glancing

at Tyler, who was watching him closely. "And we're going to find the Gold medal. *Fairly.*"

With that, Andy walked out of the restaurant. Outside, he pulled out his phone and opened *OlympiFan*. Mika joined him, a frown tugging the corners of her mouth.

"What about Emma?"

Andy stared at her. "You don't seriously want to hang out with her after that, do you?"

"I don't know." Mika shifted from one foot to the other. "She apologized. And she didn't know about A_Fan."

"Yeah, but . . ." Andy stopped, then sighed. "I guess if you want to invite her to come, it's fine."

Mika swallowed, glancing back at the restaurant. "Let's just go," she said at last. Relieved, Andy opened AR mode on his phone and started walking, keeping his eyes on the blue footprints. Someone out there was trying to cheat their way to victory. But whoever it was, they already had two hints to the Masked Medalist's identity, and they hadn't made a guess.

As long as the Gold medal was out there, Team MADR still had a chance to win the game. And if Andy couldn't win fairly, then he didn't want to win at all.

EB: Hey Mika, sorry again about Tyler. I totally get why you and Andy are upset about the notes. I just wanted to show you the message the hacker left in our team chat room . . . "I saw you leave those fake clues. Thanks for the hints, cheaters. 😎" I have no idea how this person even got into my account. So be careful, and good luck finding the Gold!

MK: Thanks! That's really nice of you. Hope we see you around soon!

EB: ☺

CHAPTER EIGHTEEN
MIKA

"HI, LILY! HI, PO!"

On Mika's phone screen, Riley giggled as she tried to lift Lily's paw in a wave. Po squirmed in Riley's lap, his big brown eyes focused on something off-screen. With an excited bark, he wiggled out of Riley's grasp and bounded off. Riley threw up her arms in defeat as Lily scampered after him.

"I tried," she said with a shrug. "But I think they heard Mom making breakfast. They know they can get her to 'accidentally' drop a couple of blueberries."

"I can't compete with that," Mika said, giggling. She was stretched out on her twin bed, already in her pajamas. On the other side of the closed door, she could hear Andy talking to Devon about the clues they'd collected that day. Mika still had no idea what the random numbers meant. Together, Andy and Mika had filled their teammates in on the confrontation with Emma, and the texts she'd sent Mika later. After discussing it, Team MADR had agreed to put the weirdness behind them. Someone out there was trying to cheat, but none of them had any idea who it might be. So they were going to focus on finding the Gold medal—and getting the hints they needed to figure out which Olympic athlete was the Masked Medalist.

"You're going to a fencing match tomorrow, right?" Riley asked, stifling a yawn. "I'm *so* jealous. I'm reading this fantasy book and last night I got to this part with the most amazing sword-fighting scene ever. It'd be awesome to see something like that in person."

"I can't wait," Mika said. "Do you think you'll be able to watch it on TV?"

"Dunno. But you'll take pictures, won't you?" Riley waggled her eyebrows. "Maybe get another billion Instagram followers, Miss Superfamous Enspire Photographer?"

Mika made a face, half-pleased, half-embarrassed. "Are you kidding? I'm lucky my parents are still letting me go watch events at all, after what I did. If they thought I was still posting on Instagram, they'd probably take my phone away forever and lock me up in our hotel room for the rest of the trip!"

"They haven't even made you delete the account," Riley pointed out. "Maybe they won't! Maybe they'll change their rule!"

"Doubt it." But Mika couldn't help feeling a twinge of hope at Riley's words. "So what are you—"

She was cut off when the door flew open and Andy burst into the room, phone in one hand, Dad's laptop precariously balancing in the other.

"Did you see this?"

He waved his phone at Mika, who blinked.

"See what?"

Andy sat on the edge of Mika's bed. He set the laptop down and turned it to face her. On the screen, she saw Devon, bleary-eyed under his Dodgers baseball cap, eating a bowl of cereal.

"Hi again," Mika said, turning her phone so that Riley could see Devon, too. Mouth full, he waved in response. "What's going on?"

"Tyler and Emma posted on the *OlympiFan* forum," Andy replied before reading from his screen. "'Fellow players: After we found the Bronze, one of our accounts was hacked and someone saw the hints to the Masked Medalist's identity that came with the medal. There is a player out there trying to cheat their way to victory—but we can level the playing field. Here are the hints that came with the Bronze medal. May the best player win.'"

Andy turned his phone so that Mika and Riley could see what was below the message:

"Whoa," Mika said, mouth open. "I can't believe Emma and Tyler did that."

Crunching his cereal, Devon nodded in agreement. "I still think leaving those notes was a weird thing to do, but they seem really into the whole fair play thing."

"Is that a butterfly?" Riley asked, and Mika moved her phone closer to Andy's so her friend could get a better look.

"It is," Andy confirmed. "A butterfly and the United Kingdom's flag."

"So does this mean the Masked Medalist is a Team GB athlete?" Mika asked eagerly. "And they, um . . . like butterflies? *Oh!* Andy, remember Paola? The cyclist at dinner the other night? She's the one who found my phone—Mom said her nickname is Signorina Butterfly!" She expected Andy to look excited, or at least interested. But he just wrinkled his nose. "What's wrong?"

"Well . . . maybe these are just more fake clues," Andy said. "The notes were fake, after all."

Riley winced. "Oh . . . I didn't think about that."

"I don't know," Mika said slowly. "That strategy was weird, but Emma and Tyler definitely seem to hate cheating. I don't think they'd go this far."

"And this is different from the notes," Devon added. "It's actually in the app. The Masked Medalist can see this message; if these aren't really the hints that came with the Bronze medal, the Masked Medalist would probably disqualify Team Cryptic, right?"

Andy perked up. "Good point!" he said, thumbs

already flying over his screen. "Let's see if the Masked Medalist posted anything about this on Instagram yet . . ." He stared, brow furrowing in confusion. Mika leaned over to see his screen and gasped.

"So? Did they post?" Riley asked eagerly. Mika and Andy exchanged a dumbstruck look.

"No," Mika said, still unable to believe what she was looking at. "The Masked Medalist's posts are all gone."

TEAM SUPERFAN CHAT ROOM

AgentAngel: Ummmm have you guys checked Instagram?

IronMatt: No, why? Another MM post?

AgentAngel: No . . .

SabineTheGreat: OMG!! They deleted all of their posts???

CHAPTER NINETEEN
ANDY

RANDOM NUMBERS DANCED in Andy's vision. He saw them in his dreams, and they didn't disappear when he woke up. He saw them while he brushed his teeth, he saw them while he ate his tamagoyaki for breakfast at the hotel, and he saw them in the taxi with Mom and Mika. Now, he even saw them as he sat in a dark arena, waiting for the next fencing match to begin. *38. 321. 207. 96.* Team MADR had collected hundreds of them, and all the app did was sort them into a vertical line that just grew longer and longer and, to Andy, still had no meaning at all.

But they had to mean *something.* This was Andy's last chance at figuring out once and for all who was behind *OlympiFan* and winning the beta tester spots. He tried to distract himself by thinking about the two hints Emma and Tyler had posted instead. A butterfly and a UK flag. The flag could mean the athlete was from the UK, or it could mean they competed in the Summer Games in London. As for the butterfly, Devon had spent some of their points on Paola Mazzanti's video in the Gallery, while Riley had read dozens of interviews with the cyclist. They couldn't find anything indicating she might have designed *OlympiFan*. But Linda McDouglas was British and Chiang Li had competed in London in 2012, so they were still at the top of Andy's list.

"This is *so* cool," Mika said, half standing out of her seat. They were in the first row near the center of the long, white strip that Mom said was called a *piste*. The ground was marked off with lines and illuminated with blue and pink lights like something out of a sci-fi movie. On either end, two women stood just in the shadows, wearing white jackets, pants, and gloves, and holding a mask and a saber.

"It is!" Wesley agreed. He and Hana were seated next to Andy and Mika. Wesley stood too, holding up his phone and taking a picture of the piste.

"Hey, you found your phone!" Mika said as Wesley sat back down. "Where was it?"

"Emi found it in the kitchen at Chef Abe's restaurant," Wesley told her, shaking his head. "I still can't believe it."

"I can," Hana said dryly. "We did take a tour of the kitchen, after all. And you have a bad habit of leaving your phone lying around."

"I didn't put it down next to the *stove*." Wesley let out a huffy sigh. "Seriously. You don't think I'm *that* careless, do you?"

Andy and Mika laughed as Hana gave Wesley a look that clearly said she thought he was exactly that: careless.

Andy heard the announcer introduce the fencers—one from Italy, the other from Russia—but then he zoned out again, picturing numbers stacked on top of one another. If only there were a pattern to figure out! Like the Fibonacci sequence, where each number was the sum of the previous two. Or if they were all prime numbers, or if each were squared or cubed or . . .

Andy sighed, rubbing his eyes. There *was* a pattern, but it was the simplest one: numerical order. When he found the clue 135, the app slotted it between 132 and 138. And when he found 133, it was slotted between 132 and 135. He had no doubt that 134 was out there somewhere, and if his team found it, it would slot before 135. So far, Riley had found the highest number—321. How many clues were out there? Andy imagined collecting thousands of them, a ridiculously long line of numbers counting up and hinting at nothing.

No one would ever find the Gold medal, and the Masked Medalist's identity would remain a secret. Maybe it would be a secret forever, seeing as they had deleted all of their Instagram posts. Andy fidgeted in his seat. *Why* had the Masked Medalist done that? Was it supposed to be a part of the game, another hint?

He felt his phone vibrate with a text and pulled it out of his pocket.

DC: HEY I finally got into the Imperial Palace Gardens and got a ton more clues, all just more numbers . . . EXCEPT

DP: @

DP: !!!

Glancing around, Andy held his breath as he responded.

AK: ???

DP: @

DP: That was the clue! Instead of a number! Must mean something, right? It's the only symbol we've found!

AK: Where does the app sort it in the line?

DP: Between 242 and 255

AK: Ok

AK: Definitely means something

DP: BUT WHAT???

Andy frowned, slipping his phone back into his pocket.

"Nine minutes on the clock," Wesley said suddenly, pointing to a digital clock at the end of the piste. "You know, I've never actually been to a fencing match before?"

"Really? I think this is one of the most exciting sports to watch in person," Hana replied. "It's a duel, but so graceful—sometimes I feel like I'm watching two people dancing, not fighting."

"What are the rules?" Mika asked, leaning forward.

"The match lasts for three bouts, three minutes each," Hana explained. "*Or* until one competitor scores fifteen points—a point for every touch they land on their opponent."

"What if time's up and they're tied?" Wesley asked.

"A minute is added to the clock, and the first to score wins."

"Even if it doesn't add up to fifteen?"

Andy scrunched his nose. An idea was trying to form in his mind . . . But then the athletes were taking their places on opposite ends of the piste, and whatever realization Andy had been about to make vanished. A hush fell over the crowd as the match began.

For the next eight minutes, Andy forgot all about *OlympiFan* and the Masked Medalist. Two competitors, dressed all in white with mesh masks hiding their faces, took their places under the lights. At the signal, their silver sabers flashed as they darted back and forth on the piste in what looked like part duel, part choreographed dance—it really *was* like something out of a movie, only way cooler.

As the clock counted down the last thirty seconds with

both athletes at thirteen points, the entire crowd seemed to hold its collective breath. Andy watched, mesmerized, as the competitors moved even faster, swiping, lunging, and dodging one another's blows—

Bing! A chime sounded, and both athletes, breathing heavily, dropped their arms and walked back to the opposite ends of the *piste*.

"Thirteen-thirteen," Wesley said, his voice rising over the crowd's excited chatter. "And there's the extra minute on the clock. So forget about fifteen total—whoever gets the next point wins, right?"

Hana rubbed her hands together gleefully. "That's right. Sudden death."

Andy sat very still, because there it was again—the answer to the numbers puzzle was trying to form in his mind, but he couldn't quite grasp it. He watched as the two athletes got into their starting positions once again.

Bing!

Both darted forward, their moves faster than ever, almost desperate as the seconds counted down. Mika squeezed Andy's arm hard, but he was too captivated by the match to pull away.

It happened so quickly that Andy barely saw it: the Italian fencer's saber slipped past the Russian athlete's attempt to block it, swiping her ribs. A buzzer sounded, and the crowd erupted into cheers as the Italian athlete pulled off her mask. She was covered in sweat, damp hair sticking to her forehead, and a huge smile stretched across her cheeks as she shook her opponent's hand. Hana let out another one of her piercing whistles, and Mika giggled as Wesley clamped his hands over her ears.

But Andy was staring at the scoreboard, which read 14–13. *Forget about fifteen total,* Wesley had said. In sudden death, the number fifteen didn't matter—it just came down to who scored the last point. Maybe the exact highest number didn't matter in the clues for the Gold medal, either.

"*Ooh.*" The word escaped Andy's lips as the applause around him grew louder. Mika turned as he whipped out his phone again.

"What's wrong?" she asked, watching as he opened *OlympiFan* to look at their team's collection of clues. It was just as Devon had described:

278

261

255

@

242

239

226

"An *at* symbol?" Mika said, leaning in closer. "Whoa, that's new."

"Devon found it." Andy looked at his sister, thinking hard. "It's between two forty-two and two fifty-five."

"Okay. What does that mean?"

Andy drummed his fingers on his knee. "Our team has almost two hundred seventy clues—all numbers except for the *at* symbol. And the highest number is three twenty-one."

"Right . . ."

"Whatever the highest number clue out there is, it can't be that much higher than the one we found," Andy said, speaking faster now. "Think about it—we found two hundred seventy random numbers, all under three twenty-one. If the clues went up to a thousand, or even higher, odds are we would've found at least a few much higher numbers, right? It's probability! The more clues we collected, the closer we got to the highest number."

"So you think three twenty-one is the highest number?"

"It's probably not the *exact* highest number, but I bet it's close." Andy closed *OlympiFan* and opened his browser. "We don't need the highest number to solve this. What are some of the tallest structures in Tokyo?"

He typed in the words as he said them, tilting his phone so that Mika could see the screen and tapping on the first result. Andy recognized the building immediately.

"The Skytree!" Mika said excitedly. "It's six hundred thirty-four meters tall."

"Okay . . ." Andy scrolled down his screen, stopping

on another familiar image—a structure that looked like a red-and-white Eiffel Tower. "Tokyo Tower. And it's . . ." Andy paused. "It's three hundred thirty-three meters tall."

Mika exhaled. "Okay. What about the *at* symbol?"

"There's an observation deck that's two hundred fifty meters high," Andy read off the screen. "Mika—I think that's what the *at* symbol means! The medal is *at* two hundred fifty meters! *It's on the observation deck!*"

Andy and Mika stared at one another for a second. Then they both shot out of their seats at the same time.

"Mom?!"

Nearly half an hour later, Dad met Andy and Mika outside of the stadium.

"Thank you, thank you, *thank you!*" Mika cried as he flagged down a taxi. "It's too far for us to go by ourselves, and Mom had to stay and work, and we know you're working, too, but we—"

"It's fine," Dad said, laughing at Mika's ramble. The taxi door opened and Dad gestured for them to get in. "I needed a break from writing anyway. And I want to be there when you guys win this thing!"

Andy's pulse quickened at the thought. He fastened his seat belt, then checked *OlympiFan* for the dozenth time in the last few minutes. "We both got in line in VR mode," he told Dad. "So did Devon and Riley, but it's after midnight in LA. They probably won't be able to stay up long enough to—"

Waving his hands, Dad chuckled again. "Honestly, this is better. After all, it was on our list of things to do!"

The drive took an excruciating twenty minutes. Andy kept refreshing *OlympiFan*, and he felt a surge of panic when he saw TilerMyths among the list of VR players in line. If Tyler knew where the Gold medal was, then so did Emma. What if she got there first?

"I hope there isn't a line for tickets," Mika said.

Dad turned around to face them. "It's a pretty popular tourist attraction, so chances are it's going to be busy."

Andy groaned.

"Which is why," Dad continued with a grin, "I already bought our tickets online."

"Yesss!" Andy and Mika exclaimed together. "Thanks, Dad!" Andy added.

"Whoops." Mika examined her shirt, frowning. "One of my pins fell off."

Andy looked down at the floor and spotted a glint of gold. "Is that it?"

"Yes!" Mika picked it up. "Oh, the butterfly. My favorite."

"Butterfly?" Andy repeated loudly. "Wait, who gave you that?"

"It's one of the pins James gave me." Mika's mouth fell open. "The hint!"

She held the pin out, and Andy took a closer look at the two bright pink wings. "I think it's a logo," Andy said. "Dad, do you recognize it?"

Dad glanced at the pin in Mika's palm. "Actually, yes! It's a Japanese company called Butterfly—they make table tennis equipment. Your mom got one of their tote bags when she interviewed Chiang Li the other day. I believe they sponsor him."

Chiang Li. Andy could tell Mika was thinking the same thing he was. But beneath his excitement, Andy felt a fresh surge of panic. Gavin Driscoll had told them that a lot of the other teams already suspected Chiang Li was the Masked Medalist. It definitely seemed like all signs pointed to him.

But Andy wanted to be absolutely positive. They *had* to get those Gold medal hints!

"Look, there it is!" Mika squealed, pointing. Andy leaned over to see through her window.

Tokyo Tower appeared as they neared the end of the block, although all Andy could see was the bright red metal base. But he knew that somewhere up there, the Gold medal waited.

In front of Tokyo Tower, Andy and Mika leapt from the taxi as soon as Dad had paid the driver. Andy glanced down the street and groaned.

"Mika, look!"

A little more than a block away, a group of people were charging down the sidewalk, whooping and yelling, all wearing neon wigs and waving miniature flags.

"Team SuperFan!" Mika cried, hopping up and down anxiously. "Dad, *hurry!*"

Andy and Mika raced to the entrance. Dad right behind them. Inside, Andy scanned the lobby and spotted the elevators, where there was a short line.

"Run!" Dad yelped.

Mika let out a wild giggle as Dad sprinted across the lobby. Andy couldn't help but laugh too, especially when they reached the line and Dad doubled over, wheezing in an exaggerated way.

"Here they come," Mika said as Team SuperFan charged into the lobby like a pack of bulls, Sabine in the lead. The elevator arrived and Andy crossed his fingers behind his back as the line shuffled forward. A woman in a pink blazer stood by the elevator, scanning tickets on each person's phone before allowing them to enter. If Andy, Mika, and Dad could fit in this elevator, they'd get to the observation deck a few minutes before Team SuperFan. But if they had to share the next elevator . . .

"Yesss!" Mika cheered again when they managed to squeeze inside. Andy caught a glimpse of the rival team running toward them, but they were too late.

"Oops. Should we have waited for them?" Dad said teasingly as the doors slid closed.

"Noooo!" said Andy and Mika, both laughing. Andy's heart was pounding with excitement. They had a head start—maybe they really could find the Gold first!

The ride up to the top took a few minutes, but it felt like hours. When the doors finally opened, Andy and Mika spilled out—and stumbled to a shocked halt.

Sunshine streamed into the circular atrium through the curved glass wall, and beyond that, Andy could see buildings spread out far below them. The view was incredible, but that wasn't what had caught Andy and Mika's attention.

Emma Botha stood a few feet away, her phone out as she scanned the atrium through her screen. When she spotted the Kudos, she lowered her phone, her mouth open in surprise. Andy's brain felt jammed. She'd beaten them here—but she hadn't found the Gold medal.

Yet.

Her lips twitched into a smile, and for some reason, Andy found himself smiling back. *May the best player win,* he thought.

"*Wow*—that view really is worth it!" Dad said cheerfully, oblivious to the staring contest happening right in front of him. "Sooo . . . where should we start—"

"This way!" Andy dashed off to the left, while

Emma sprinted in the opposite direction. Dad jogged to keep up as Andy and Mika scoured the atrium through their screens, looking for any sign of a virtual medal.

When Andy spotted the elevators again, he tried to ignore a wave of frustration. The footprints at the bottom of his screen were still blue. But the medal had to be here. It *had* to.

"Wait, that isn't the same elevator we came up in." Mika said suddenly.

"It probably goes up to the other observation deck," Dad said, and Andy and Mika stared at him.

"There's *two*? I thought we were on the top already!"

Dad consulted the screen of his phone where their tickets were pulled up on his screen. "Yep. I bought tickets for both. This one is a hundred fifty meters high. The other one is a hundred meters higher."

Andy and Mika looked at one another. *Two hundred fifty meters.*

"Hurry!" Andy ran toward the elevator with Mika and Dad.

"I have to admit, this game is pretty exciting!" Dad said breathlessly as he followed them, showing the woman their tickets on his phone.

Despite his nerves, Andy was smiling. It *was* exciting. This felt better than when they had been at the zoo. If Andy found the medal this time, it would be fair and not because they had a sneaky advantage over the other players. This was *way* more fun.

They hurried off the elevator, and Andy blinked in astonishment. This deck was smaller, but even more impressive, with shiny white floors, angled mirrors on the walls and ceiling, and cool purple lights below the windows. The view of the city from this high was dizzying, but Andy told himself there would be time to appreciate it after they won the Gold. He and Mika moved quickly, holding out their phones.

"Hurry!" Mika yelled, running around the corner. Andy followed her, summoning an extra burst of speed like a marathoner on the final lap, darting between a few tourists like a fencer dodging a blow. In front of him, Mika leapt over a bright pink backpack as nimbly as a hurdler. A little girl by the windows clapped her hands to her mouth in awe as they charged past. Andy glanced at his screen and let out a triumphant cry.

The footprints were gold.

"We're close!" His hand shook slightly as he slowed, sweeping his phone from side to side. Behind him, he heard a *ding!* and glanced over his shoulder just as Emma and Team SuperFan spilled out of the elevator. Andy checked the floor, the ceiling, the windows . . . the footprints glowed pink, and he stumbled to a sudden halt, spinning on the spot. Something flickered on his screen, and for a split second, he thought it was the sun's reflection. Then his mouth went dry.

The Gold medal hovered at eye level by the window against the backdrop of a clear blue sky.

Andy didn't hesitate. He tapped the medal, and it zoomed toward him until his whole screen was a brilliant gold. A moment later, confetti exploded, revealing a message that shimmered and sparkled.

Found by AndyK (AR)

Congratulations to the Gold Medalists: TEAM MADR!!!

Exhaling, Andy felt a grin spread across his face. He heard Mika squeal, and then came distant groans and cries of dismay from Team SuperFan.

"What's going on?" Dad asked.

Andy turned around just as Mika threw her arms around him. "We did it!" she hollered, squeezing him so hard he yelped. "Oh, sorry!"

She pulled away, beaming, and Andy beamed back. Then he spotted Emma a few feet away, rubbing a stitch in her side and trying to catch her breath. She flashed him another little smile.

"You found it! Congrats!"

"Thanks." Andy still couldn't believe it. He looked at his phone, where a new message waited.

Choose one!
750 points + 2 hints
1,000 points + 1 hint

Team MADR had been in total agreement about this choice. The only way to win the grand prize—to become beta testers—was to correctly guess the Masked Medalist's identity. And to do that, they'd need all the hints they could get. Andy selected the first option, and the message closed.

"Let's see those hints!" Mika cried eagerly, swiping her screen. "Ooh, there's the medal!"

Andy could see it on his screen, too—a shiny Gold medal at the top right under *Team MADR*.

"Just tap the medal and you'll see your hints," Emma said, hanging back. "Don't worry, I won't look!"

Andy looked at her, wondering if he should share their hints with her and Tyler. After all, Team Cryptic shared their hints with all the other players.

"Numbers," Mika said, eyes shining as she looked up from her screen. "And Emma's hints were pictures.

Team SuperFan's hint was probably a sound clip."

Quickly, Andy tapped the Gold medal, and he saw what Mika meant.

2012
2

Andy grinned. *Four* hints. They were going to figure out who the Masked Medalist was and become beta testers and work with an actual Olympic athlete. He couldn't believe it.

"Any idea what it means?" Dad asked. "Maybe they competed in the 2012 Olympics?" His phone suddenly rang, and he glanced at the screen. "Ah, it's Emi—I need to take this. I'll be right over there, okay?"

"Okay!" As Dad walked over to a quiet spot near the windows, Andy turned to Mika. "Chiang Li competed in 2012, but the number two . . . two medals, maybe? We have to research! Do you think Devon and Riley are still awake?"

"I was just checking the chat room!" Mika did a little happy dance. But a moment later, she fell still. "Uh . . . this is weird."

"What?"

"There's a new message in the chat room . . . from *me*. But I didn't type it."

"*What?*" Andy opened the chat room to see for himself. Mika held out her phone to Emma, who moved closer.

Mika: Thanks for the hints! 😎

"That's the cheater!" Emma said in a low voice. "That looks just like the message they left when my account was hacked!"

Mika looked dumbstruck. "It just popped up a few seconds ago. So this person was in my account?"

She looked from Andy to Emma. Then the three of them turned to look at where a few of the Team Super-Fan players were staring glumly at their phones. Sabine pulled off her aqua wig, her blond hair sticking up from static electricity.

"They won the Silver," Emma said quietly. "And whoever's trying to cheat saw the hints from the Bronze and the Gold."

Andy knew what she was thinking. The hacker might be standing just a few feet away. And they could have all the hints.

OLYMPIFAN UPDATE!

Special message from the Masked Medalist

Congratulations to our Gold medalists, Team MADR!
But fear not, OlympiFans—our game isn't over yet.

The grand prize is still up for grabs.

Each team gets **ONE** chance to guess my identity,
so guess wisely.

WHO IS THE MASKED MEDALIST?

SCOREBOARD - TOP TEN

1st	⭐	MADR	1,437
2nd	⭐	SuperFan	1,351
3rd	⭐	Cryptic	866
4th		TheOracles	578
5th		野心	566
6th		MysticMice	552
7th		베스트	549
8th		ALLEYOOP	547
9th		Rabenklaue	542
10th		DragonFlame	540

CHAPTER TWENTY

MIKA

MIKA STARED HARD at Sabine and her friends huddled together near the wall, looking at their phones and whispering. Had one of them hacked into her account? It was hard to imagine—after all, they'd just witnessed Andy finding the medal. Now they were standing right over there, looking more glum than guilty. Maybe they were really good actors.

Or maybe they weren't trying to cheat at all.

"*No!*"

Sabine cried out in alarm, and everyone on the deck turned to stare. A second later, her team members began to argue loudly, pointing at their phones and gesturing accusingly at one another. Mika checked her phone, positive another team had guessed the Masked Medalist's identity and won the grand prize, but there was no update.

"What's going on?"

"Let's find out." Emma walked past her, heading

toward the distraught teens. Andy and Mika exchanged a glance before following her. Sabine looked up in surprise at Emma, who crossed her arms. "What happened?" Emma demanded.

Sabine looked from her to Andy and Mika, and she attempted to smile as she stepped away from her teammates. "Congratulations, guys!" she said. "Did you go for two hints, or more points?"

Mika stared at her. Something about Sabine's expression was off. She'd always been cheerful and friendly before, but now she seemed . . . guarded. What was she hiding?

"Hints," Andy replied. "Is something wrong? You all look really upset."

Sabine heaved a sigh. "Well, actually . . . *OlympiFan* says we took our guess and got it wrong."

"Whaat?" Mika hadn't been expecting that.

"But we didn't guess!" insisted a boy in a lime-green hat. He looked around at his teammates, his eyes wide. "Right? No one entered a guess!"

The other four nodded, then fell into a loud discussion. Sabine took another step away from her friends. "I guess I'm glad we went with one hint and more points when we won the Silver," she said. "The behind-the-scenes videos in the Gallery are really cool."

"Someone on your team tried to make a guess with just one hint? That's pretty risky." Emma lowered her voice. "Unless one of them is the cheater and had *five* hints because they'd been in *our* accounts."

Sabine looked taken aback. "What? No!"

"Are you sure?" Andy asked. "Because someone hacked into our account a few minutes ago and saw our hints, just like they did to Team Cryptic when they won the Bronze." He gestured to Emma, who nodded. "Your team is the only one the cheater left alone."

Mika could tell that Sabine was starting to get upset. "My friends are not cheaters, and neither am I. In fact . . ." Sabine swiped her phone, then held it out. Mika saw a sound clip icon on the screen. "This is the hint to the Masked Medalist's identity that came with the Silver medal," Sabine said. "Play it."

Mika looked from Andy to Emma. No one moved.

"Go on, seriously," said Sabine earnestly. "Team Cryptic played fair. So does Team SuperFan. Whoever's cheating won't have an advantage if everyone has all the hints, so play it!"

After a second, Andy reached out and tapped *play*.

BEEZZT!

The clip was only a second long, but it was definitely familiar. It sounded like a cross between a *beep* and a *buzz*. Mika had heard it before—but where?

Sabine lowered her phone. "I'll post this for all the players to have, just like you did," she told Emma. Then she turned back to Mika and Andy. "Okay?"

Mika nodded. "Thank you."

"Yeah, thanks," Andy echoed. "And we'll post ours, too." He looked at Mika. "Right? It's only fair."

"Yeah, definitely," Mika said emphatically, and Andy started typing on his phone. A moment later, he held it up.

"There. I posted ours in the *OlympiFan* forums."

"That *is* fair," Sabine said, smiling at them before returning to her friends. Mika watched as Team SuperFan headed to the ramp. Something was nagging at her, but she couldn't figure it out.

"Mika."

She turned to see Andy staring at his phone as if it might explode any second.

"What if the cheater *did* get into Team SuperFan's account?" he said. "If they're all telling the truth about not entering a guess about the Masked Medalist, someone else did it. What if the cheater got them disqualified by making a wrong guess?"

Mika gasped. "Oh—they could do that to us, too!"

"Change your password," Emma said immediately. "Hurry!"

"I'm going to tell Devon and Riley to do it, too," Mika added, navigating to the chat room as she spoke. "Just in case."

"I'll change mine, too," Andy said.

Mika finished her post to Devon and Riley, then

opened her *OlympiFan* account information. She entered her old password, then typed in a new one and tapped *change.*

The password you entered is incorrect.

"What?" Mika frowned at her phone and tried again, only to see the same message. "Um . . . the app says my old password is wrong."

Andy looked at her screen. "That's weird. Are you sure you entered the right one?"

"Yes . . . well, pretty sure." Mika had set up her *Olympi-Fan* account weeks ago and never logged out. "What do I do now?"

"Log out and then tap *forgot my password,*" Emma suggested. "Then it'll send a link to your email and you can reset it even if you don't remember your old one."

Mika hesitated, then tapped *log out.* She was pretty positive she *did* remember her old password, but it wouldn't do any good to argue.

"I still don't understand how the cheater got into your accounts in the first place," Andy said. "Were your passwords that easy to guess?"

"Mine definitely wasn't," Emma said. "It was a cryptogram. A really, really long one. No one could just guess it."

"Someone did, though." Andy pocketed his phone. "How else would they get in?"

Emma sighed. "I have no idea."

Mika could tell from Andy's expression that he was just as disappointed as she was. Whoever the cheater was, it looked like they were probably going to get away with it and maybe even win the grand prize. After all, they had five hints to the Masked Medalist's identity.

But then again, so did Mika and Andy. They just had to solve the puzzle first.

By the time the Kudos arrived at Chef Abe's restaurant that evening, Mika was relieved to have a distraction from *OlympiFan*. She'd felt anxious all day, going over and over the hints and waiting for whoever had cheated to reveal the Masked Medalist's identity and win the game. More than a dozen teams had entered their guesses— but they had all been wrong.

"Mika! Andy!"

Mika turned as Emma hopped out of a taxi that had pulled up right behind theirs. "Hi, Emma! Hi, Mrs. Botha!"

"So nice to see you again," Mrs. Botha said, then held out her hand to Dad. "Mr. and Mrs. Kudo. I understand we have you to thank for this invitation?"

"Oh, I don't think I had much to do with it," Dad told her with a grin. "Chef Abe's publicist was thrilled to have another Olympic athlete on the guest list."

As Dad spoke, a young man climbed out of the taxi.

He straightened up, and Emma grabbed him by the arm and pulled him over to the others.

"Everyone, this is my brother, Antony," she announced. "This is Mika and Andy and their parents. They were sitting with us when you won the bronze!"

Antony smiled at them. "Nice to meet you all," he said softly. He seemed to be much shyer than his sister, who clung to his arm and beamed like she might burst with pride. "I hope you've been enjoying the Games!" He glanced at Mika's purse; she'd fastened all of the pins she'd collected onto the strap. "You're a collector?" Antony asked with a smile.

Mika tried to respond, yet all that came out was a squeak. Andy seemed just as starstruck, but Mom stepped in quickly.

"It's a pleasure to meet you," she said, shaking Antony's hand. "And I have to say, your race was one of the most exciting events we had the pleasure of watching this week!"

Mom and Dad kept up a steady stream of chatter with Mrs. Botha and Antony as they crossed the lobby. Inside the elevator, Emma squeezed in next to Mika and whispered, "I think I know how the cheater got into my account."

On Mika's other side, Andy leaned closer. "How?"

Emma glanced at her mother and brother, who were still talking to Mika's parents. "Remember when we met at the shrine, I told you my mom and I had been across the street buying souvenirs? We were, but as soon as Tyler realized the clues were a photo of the Meiji Shrine, he got in the VR line then messaged me. We both knew I probably wouldn't get there in time, but he wanted me to leave the notes so other AR players would find them. I ran over to the gate and saw you guys and Team SuperFan."

"And Tyler found the medal before us in VR mode," Mika said, nodding.

"Right. And then after I left the notes and talked to you, I went back to the souvenir shop." Emma bit her lip. "Well, it didn't seem like a big deal at the time, but I lost my phone. Just for a minute—my mom found it on a shelf with some figurines I'd been looking at for my grandma."

"So you set it down and forgot about it?" Andy asked.

Emma frowned. "That's what my mom said. But the thing is, I *know* I didn't. Tyler and I had just won the Bronze. We were excited and kept texting about the hints and what they could mean. I stuck the phone in my back pocket while I was looking at the figurines. I'm positive. And it was really crowded in that shop; people kept bumping into me."

"So you think . . ." Mika paused, lowering her voice to a whisper. "You think someone took it out of your pocket?"

"Whoever got into our account saw me leaving the notes at the shrine," Emma replied quietly. "They could have followed me to the shop and taken my phone. I was logged in to my account so they didn't need my password! All they had to do was look at the hints and then leave that message in our chat room—it would only take a few seconds. Then they left my phone on the shelf."

"I don't get it," Andy said. "Tyler was positive that Mika and I were the ones who cheated, but you would have noticed if we'd followed you to the shop."

"Yeah, but we didn't even realize what had happened until later that night!" Emma exclaimed. "I didn't open the app again all day because my mom and I went to watch the equestrian event. And Tyler kept playing, but he didn't check our chat room because he knew I was busy. By the time we saw the message, I'd forgotten about misplacing my phone."

Ding! The doors slid open.

Mrs. Botha gasped as the group stepped off the elevator. "Oh my! This is lovely!"

Mika blinked as she took in the restaurant. Next to her, Emma whistled softly. "Wow."

"Seriously." Mika had forgotten how incredible Kenji was, with its 360-degree view of the city, the giant kitchen with cool mirrors and neon lights, and the boxy chandeliers that glowed in soft blues and pinks overhead. And now, with music pulsing from the speakers and a crowd of people in suits and fancy dresses, it seemed even more glamorous.

"Tom! Karen!" Emi hurried over, wearing a beautiful blue silk dress with a pattern of red roses. "Welcome—and you must be the Bothas!"

Mika hung back as the introductions were made. She glanced over her shoulder at the corridor, picturing the private room where they'd had dinner for the soft opening. The déjà vu was back, and it wasn't just because she'd been here before. Something else was nagging at the back of her mind, trying to grab her attention, but she couldn't quite figure it out.

"Kenji is more than just a restaurant," she heard Emi saying as she led them inside. "It's a place to be seen, to interact. We encourage our guests to mingle between courses. Every evening, Chef Abe will serve a nine-course meal—but the courses will always be different, depending on what's in season, what looks particularly fresh or special at the market."

Standing on tiptoe, Mika spotted the young chef moving swiftly around the kitchen in the middle of the room. Unlike the two chefs assisting him, both wearing traditional white coats and hats, Chef Abe was dressed all in black—and he wore a huge grin. From what Mika could see, he was already putting on a show for the older journalist who had sat next to Mika at the soft opening.

As Mika and Andy watched, Chef Abe tossed ingredients into a skillet with a flourish as flames shot up from the gas burners. Grabbing a spatula, he flipped a fried shrimp out of the skillet—and right into the surprised journalist's open mouth!

"Goal!" Chef Abe cried, raising his arms over his head.

Mika giggled as everyone watching burst into applause. "I guess Emi was right," she said to Andy. "Chef Abe isn't so shy when he's cooking!"

She spotted Wesley Brooks standing near the kitchen, chatting animatedly with Valentina and James. Next to Wesley, Hana Takahashi was taking video of Chef Abe's performance on her phone.

"Mika, look!" Andy pointed at a nearby table, where Gavin Driscoll was talking to an older couple. Before she could reply, he was already making his way to Gavin's table. Emma and Mika exchanged a confused look, and then followed him.

"Well, hey there, Kudo kids!" Gavin said cheerfully as the couple wandered over to another table. "I hear congratulations are in order?"

"What? Oh." Andy smiled half-heartedly. "You mean the Gold medal?"

"That's right!" Gavin looked with curiosity at Emma. "You're an *OlympiFan* player, too, right? I remember seeing you at the shrine!"

"This is Emma—she's on Team Cryptic," Mika told Gavin with a grin. "She and her friend Tyler won the Bronze."

Emma smiled as Gavin let out a whistle. "Lucky me, getting to meet all of the medalists! Say, are you three up for an interview for my documentary? Not now, but—maybe tomorrow morning? With your parents' permission, of course."

"Yeah, definitely!" Andy said. "Speaking of—you interviewed Team SuperFan, right?"

Gavin grinned. "Those goofy kids with the hats and wigs? Yup, I have lots of footage of them. Very chatty."

"This might sound weird, but . . ." Andy hesitated, glancing at Mika before continuing. "Did any of them say anything suspicious?"

"Suspicious? Like what?"

Mika knew what her brother was getting at. "There's a player out there who's cheating," she told Gavin bluntly. "They got into our account *and* Emma's account and saw the hints that came with our medals."

"And you think it was one of them?" Gavin asked. "Well, that's a shame. But I'm sorry, I don't think I can be of much help—I only really talked to them at the shrine, and that was right after this young lady's team won the Bronze." He nodded at Emma, who smiled. "Those poor kids were upset about the loss, for sure. And that one over there, he was *mad.* He thought someone was trying to cheat. He came over to me right when I got here tonight, actually—kept trying to tell me the whole game was rigged, but then Emi made him get to work."

Mika, Andy, and Emma looked in the direction Gavin was pointing, then at one another, confused. "Wait, one of the SuperFans is *here*?" Andy asked.

"Yeah, Emi's nephew, Kaito. That's him at that table over there . . ." Gavin gestured again, and Mika saw a table with three older women sipping bright-blue drinks and laughing together. She was about to ask Gavin who he was talking about when he added: "The busboy."

Mika's eyes went to a sullen-faced boy with a fringe of black hair, setting a plate of appetizers on the table. Her hand flew to her mouth.

"Emi's nephew is on Team SuperFan?" Andy asked in disbelief. "I remember her saying that he played *OlympiFan*, but I don't remember seeing him at Tokyo Tower this morning. Do you guys?"

"No, definitely not," Emma said. "Mika?"

Startled, Mika finally tore her eyes off the busboy. "No, he wasn't there," she said. "But thanks anyway, Gavin!"

She waved at Gavin, then hurried off to a nearby window. When she reached an empty table, Mika set her purse down and pulled out her phone. By the time Andy and Emma caught up, she had already started searching through her photos.

"What's going on?" Andy said, looking concerned. "You're acting weird."

"Look." Mika placed her phone flat on the table. "Here's Team SuperFan at the Giant Ghibli Clock, right when they found the Silver. How many of them are there?"

Andy and Emma leaned in closer. "Six," Emma said. "Just like this morning."

"Right." Mika began swiping until she reached the photos she'd taken at the Meiji Shrine. "But what about here?"

There was a pause. "Seven," Andy said finally. "There were seven of them."

Mika swiped again, stopping on the photo of Gavin interviewing the boy with the oversize sunglasses—and a familiar, sullen expression. Emma's mouth fell open.

"That's him—that's the busboy!"

"Are you sure?" Andy asked, leaning closer to the screen. "I mean, it does look like him, but—"

"It's him," Mika said urgently. "He was at the soft opening, too, Andy. I thought he looked familiar then, but I didn't recognize him because of those giant sunglasses." She paused, taking a deep breath. "He's the cheater."

"What?" Andy's eyes widened. "How do you know?"

"Remember how I lost my phone and I had to come back upstairs?"

"Yeah . . ."

"It was on the table under a napkin," Mika said, her voice growing louder. "And I'm absolutely positive I left it in my purse all night. He took it! He took it out of my purse, and then he left it on that table."

"But that was days ago," Andy said. "How did he get into your account this morning when we won the Gold?"

"I bet I know." Mika was already opening her email app. "Remember how *OlympiFan* kept saying I was entering the wrong password this morning? I had to log out and tell it I forgot my password to reset it. Kaito could've done the same thing . . . he *did*, look!"

She showed Andy and Emma her screen. In the trash was a deleted email sent from *OlympiFan* a week ago notifying her that she'd successfully changed her password. Mika felt a chill race up her spine. Kaito had been logged in to her account for a whole week, and she hadn't even known!

Emma shook her head. "Whoa. You're totally right. He didn't need to know your password to change it, because you were already logged in. Then he gave you a new password and logged in as you from his own phone."

"And at the shrine," Mika went on, navigating back to her photos. "See, Gavin's looking at the spot where Emma left the note because Kaito was trying to tell him about it! He must have pointed to the note right before I took the photo. He saw Emma leave it, and he followed her to the souvenir shop and took her phone, too!"

"But he didn't know I was on Team Cryptic," Emma said, chewing her lip. "Why'd he take my phone?"

"Because he thought you were cheating," Mika pointed out. "Maybe he was trying to figure out exactly what you were doing with those notes. Once Kaito had your phone and realized you were on Team Cryptic, he saw the Bronze medal and left a message saying he stole your hints."

"And then as soon as Andy found the Gold medal, he saw our hints and left that message." Mika blinked as another thought occurred to her. "And *then* he logged into *his* account with Team SuperFan and entered the wrong guess—that's why his teammates were freaking out! They probably didn't realize he was still playing!"

"I'm going to tell Sabine," Andy said, already opening *OlympiFan* on his phone.

Emma's frown deepened. "It's weird . . . Kaito had *five* hints about the Masked Medalist's identity, and he still guessed wrong! Who do you think he guessed?"

Mika crossed her arms. "Maybe we should go ask him."

From: SabineTheGreat
To: AndyK

Thanks for letting me know about Kaito. The thing is, I already knew he was the one who guessed.

I'm SO sorry for lying to you and your sister. My teammates have no idea it was Kaito, and I didn't want them to find out. Kaito's pretty new to our school—he enrolled right after winter break so he didn't have a lot of friends. None of us knew him very well before OlympiFan and he got very intense about winning.

When we were all at the Meiji Shrine, Kaito saw your friend Emma leaving notes with fake clues. He showed me and said he thought our team needed a strategy like that. I disagreed because I thought it was too sneaky. Kaito asked the team to vote—either stick to the way we were playing, or come up with a new strategy to throw off the other teams, like he wanted. Everyone voted against him. I think we hurt his feelings. We didn't mean to! Then one night he called me and said he knew who the Masked Medalist was! He said he'd seen an Olympic athlete logged in to the Masked Medalist's Instagram, typing a post. He wanted to enter the athlete's name so that Team SuperFan would win the grand prize even if we didn't find the Gold. I said no way! I didn't want to win by cheating, and I knew my friends wouldn't either. I made him promise not to tell our teammates who the athlete was. Kaito got really upset and quit. When we all saw the message on OlympiFan saying our team had taken our guess, I knew it was him. But I didn't tell anyone because I felt bad for Kaito. I really think he was just doing all of this because he thought we would like him better if he helped us win.

I'm really sorry.
Sabine

CHAPTER TWENTY-ONE

ANDY

"WAIT."

Andy put a hand on his sister's arm. Mika looked ready to storm over to the busboy and demand he confess everything—and Andy had to admit, it was a tempting thought.

But Sabine had responded so quickly. Andy scanned her message, then read it again, his mind reeling.

"What?" Mika asked, frowning at Andy. "Come on, he's right over there!"

She fell silent when Andy held his phone out. Emma leaned across the table, and Andy waited while they read Sabine's message.

"Whoa . . ." Emma said finally.

Mika looked as stunned as Andy felt. "No wonder Sabine was acting so weird at Tokyo Tower. She didn't want us to know that one of her teammates *did* try to cheat. She probably realized it was Kaito who'd made the guess, and she didn't want her friends to find out."

"One thing doesn't make sense," Emma said, looking at Andy. "If Kaito actually saw this athlete's phone and they were logged in to the Masked Medalist's Instagram, then why was his guess wrong?"

Mika chewed her lip. "Sabotage? Kaito wanted Team SuperFan to lose?"

"But Sabine said he thought the other team members would like him if he won the game for them," Emma pointed out. "And that was Kaito's only chance to win!"

"That's true," Mika agreed. "I wonder which athlete he thought it was?"

"I think I know."

Both girls turned to Andy. He gazed thoughtfully at his phone, allowing his mind to put the pieces together in a different way. At last, they were starting to fit.

"Kaito told Sabine he knew who the Masked Medalist was because he saw the athlete logged in to the Instagram account. But when he looked at the hints, they didn't make sense—remember how Gavin said Kaito thought the game was rigged? He was angry because he thought the Masked Medalist had made the game impossible to solve. I'll bet that's when he deleted the Masked Medalist's Instagram posts." Andy looked up at his sister. "He took your phone during the soft opening, Mika—but you weren't the only person who lost their phone that night."

Mika wrinkled her nose. "I wasn't? Who—oh!" she

exclaimed, her eyes widening. "Wesley did, too!"

"Wesley?" Emma asked. "You mean Wesley Brooks?"

"Yes! He told us he lost his phone that night, too," Mika said excitedly. "Then Emi found it in the kitchen. And Kaito was the busboy that night . . . wait. So this means . . ."

"Wesley Brooks is the Masked Medalist," Emma whispered. "Right?"

Andy's pulse was racing, but he forced himself to think through it one more time. "That's what Kaito thought. But when Kaito entered Wesley's name, the app said his guess was wrong."

"Well, good," Mika said, hands on her hips. "I mean, he cheated. He doesn't deserve to win."

"That's true, but telling him that we know what he did won't fix anything." Andy said. "We can't prove he did it."

Mika let out a strained laugh. "So we just let him get away with it?"

"No." Emma placed her hands flat on the table and leaned closer, her dark eyes sparkling. "We need to get him to admit it."

"How?"

Andy thought carefully, his gaze wandering over the crowd until he spotted Gavin again. "I have an idea. Let's find our parents—Gavin needs their permission to interview us. And I think we should do it tonight."

Over an hour later, Andy finished off a bowl of *okayu*—rice porridge, according to the translation on the menu—topped with salmon roe. His nervousness over what they were about to do hadn't stopped him from digging in to seven courses so far. Tonight, Chef Abe's dishes were even better than at the soft opening, and judging from everyone's reactions this evening, his restaurant was going to be a huge success.

"There he is," Mika said in a low voice, pushing her empty bowl back and picking up her soda. A few tables away, Andy spotted Kaito serving a pair of women tall, thin glasses filled with something pink and bubbly. "He's right next to Gavin—should we do it now?"

"Yeah." Andy set his napkin down, glancing around until he spotted Emma. He nodded at her, and she nodded back, then pulled her phone out. Andy and Mika headed for Gavin's table, and Emma edged toward them.

"Hi again!" Mika said cheerfully, plopping her soda down on the table. "We were wondering if we could do that interview about *OlympiFan* now."

Out of the corner of his eye, Andy saw Kaito glance over at them. "We think we figured out who the Masked Medalist is." Andy made sure to say it loudly, and sure enough, Kaito froze, still clutching his tray.

Gavin's eyebrows shot up, and he pushed back his plate of spicy crab legs. "Did you now? I'd love to hear about it."

He reached down and pulled his camera out from a bag underneath the table. A chorus of *oohs* and *aahs* rose up nearby, and the warm, sweet scent of chocolate filled the air as Chef Abe began his dessert presentation. Andy stepped closer to Mika, and Gavin began to record.

"Mika and Andy Kudo found the Gold medal at Tokyo Tower this morning," Gavin said. "And now, they believe they've solved the mystery of the Masked Medalist's identity!"

Kaito wasn't the only person listening now. While most of the crowd was still captivated by Chef Abe and his dessert show, Andy noticed that the people at nearby tables had started to watch their interview with curiosity.

"Not just us," Mika said as Emma joined them, holding her phone out. On her screen, Tyler waved at Gavin. "This is Emma Botha, and that's Tyler Smith," Mika explained. "They're Team Cryptic—they found the Bronze medal and the first two hints to the Masked Medalist's identity."

"When someone hacked into my *OlympiFan* account and saw the two hints, we shared them with all of the other players," Emma added loudly. "Because we think games are only fun when they're fair for everyone."

"The same person got into my account right after Andy found the Gold medal," Mika added. "They saw our two hints, too."

"Well, that's a pretty sneaky thing to do," Gavin said.

"And what about the Silver medal? Do you think this person did the same thing to the team who found it?"

Andy shrugged. "Maybe. It doesn't matter, because obviously the cheater still doesn't know who the Masked Medalist is. But we do."

He crossed his fingers behind his back, trying hard not to look at Kaito. Would he fall for their trap?

"Well?" Gavin asked eagerly. "Who is it?"

Andy took a deep breath, glancing at Mika, Emma, and Tyler. All four of them spoke at the same time.

"Wesley Brooks."

The restaurant had grown quiet, and Andy glanced at the island kitchen. Several fondue pots sat on the bar as Chef Abe torched a tray lined with marshmallows. He was making a show of it, doing a little flourish with the torch before moving from one marshmallow to the next. But the attention wasn't on him anymore, even when he increased the flames. Everyone was looking either at Gavin's table, or at Wesley Brooks.

"Sorry, guys."

Wesley stepped forward. He was smiling in an apologetic way, hands in his pockets.

Gavin swiveled around to get Wesley on camera. "So you're not the Masked Medalist?"

Andy held his breath.

"Afraid not," said Wesley, and from behind Gavin came a shout of anger.

"Yes you are!"

Kaito stalked over, hands curled into fists. Andy watched as the busboy walked right up to Wesley.

"Kaito!" Emi stepped through the crowd, her expression alarmed. "What's going on?"

Wesley looked calm, although his smile was gone. "I'm sorry, but—"

"It's you!" Kaito insisted. "You posted a picture on the Masked Medalist's Instagram account before dinner here last week. I took your phone and saw it! But when I entered your name in the *OlympiFan* app, it said I was wrong! My team should have won the grand prize!"

"Whoa . . . You took my phone that night?" Wesley shook his head. "Man, I thought I was losing my mind. And buddy, I don't think you deserve to win since you clearly cheated."

Kaito scowled. "*You* cheated! You're the Masked Medalist!"

Hana appeared behind Wesley, watching Kaito closely. Emi looked beside herself with embarrassment. Chef Abe began stirring a vat of chocolate vigorously, eyeing the busboy who now had the attention of the entire restaurant.

Wesley sighed. "I'm really sorry," he said, sounding like he meant it. "But I'm afraid you've made a mistake. It's true, I run the Masked Medalist's Instagram, but I didn't *create the game.* You guessed wrong. Didn't you consider the hints?"

Andy inhaled sharply as he thought about the five hints again. The UK flag. A butterfly. 2012. 2. And that sound, that *beezzt*—a sound he'd heard just a few days ago at the swimming events. It was the starting buzzer that signaled the beginning of a race.

Swimmer. Butterfly. London. 2012. Two gold medals.

Andy had been so focused on getting Kaito to confess, he'd forgotten to put the last puzzle piece into place! His gaze moved from Wesley to Hana Takahashi as everything finally clicked. When she noticed him staring at her, she smiled and stepped forward.

"You have to type it into the app to win," she said quietly.

Swallowing hard, Andy looked from Mika to Emma and Tyler. He was sorely tempted to pull out his phone, but he didn't.

"No," he said at last. "I only figured it out because Wesley said he runs the Masked Medalist's Instagram. And since I know you're friends, that's a really big hint the other players didn't have. I don't want to win this way—it's not fair to the other teams."

"And the game was totally fair until *someone* started stealing phones and changing passwords," Mika added, glaring pointedly at Kaito.

The busboy looked shell-shocked as all eyes turned to

him. Even Chef Abe was staring, his mouth a round O of surprise at this turn of events. Kaito blinked, looking from Hana to Wesley to Gavin—and at the sight of Gavin's camera, he seemed to realize what had just happened.

With a frightened cry, he pushed past Gavin, who stepped out of the way too quickly and began to lose his balance. His giant camera knocked against Kaito's shoulder, and the busboy stumbled toward the kitchen— heading right for the beautiful chocolate fountain.

"*No!*" Chef Abe lunged forward to protect the chocolate fountain, throwing his arms wide, and slamming into a large mixing bowl filled with fluffy whipped cream. The bowl soared high into the air and turned over. Chef Abe looked up as it began to fall—straight toward his head.

There was a collective gasp from the crowd, and Andy heard Emi let out a shriek of dismay. Kaito shoved the chef out of the way, and the bowl landed squarely on top of his head instead.

"Kaito!" Emi hurried forward. "Oh, goodness. Are you okay?"

The busboy gingerly lifted the bowl. His hair, his face, and his neck were completely covered in whipped cream. Andy heard a few giggles, which were quickly stifled. He felt bad for Kaito, but he couldn't help feeling relieved that Chef Abe hadn't been humiliated on his opening night.

Apparently, Chef Abe felt the same way. Regaining his composure, he stepped forward and gave Kaito a little bow. Then he clapped the busboy on the back and smiled widely at the rapt audience. "My desserts are delicious, but please resist the urge to swim in them," he joked.

The tension in the room broke, and everyone laughed. Andy could have sworn he even saw Kaito crack a small smile beneath all the whipped cream.

Emi was clearly relieved. "Ladies and gentlemen, I'm so sorry for this, but—"

"But the show must go on," Chef Abe finished grandly. Then he struck a match and tossed it into the vat of cherries, sending streaks of flame into the air.

Applause broke out, and Emi put her arm around Kaito and led him out of the room. Andy let out a long sigh of relief and then turned to Mika and Emma. On the screen, Tyler was grinning.

"I can't believe that worked!"

Andy was about to reply, but the words caught in his throat when Wesley and Hana joined them.

"I think we have a lot to talk about," Hana said with a wide smile.

"And a lot of dessert to eat," Wesley added. "Although I think they might be out of whipped cream . . ."

OLYMPIFAN UPDATE!
Special message from the Masked Medalist

Hello, OlympiFans! The Closing Ceremony is tonight—
and our game has come to an end as well.
But wait, what about the grand prize? No one has
guessed who the Masked Medalist is!

Well, that's not entirely true. You might have seen rumors
swirling around on social media last night that the
Masked Medalist had been unmasked. And it's true!
I, Hana Takahashi, created OlympiFan.
So, who guessed my identity? Who won the grand prize?
Well, that's a little bit more complicated.

I designed OlympiFan to be both fun and fair. And while it
was definitely fun (for me, and I hope for all of you, too!),
it didn't turn out to be totally fair. While it's true that a
player was attempting to cheat, I'm taking responsibility
for this. I have lots of other games in the works, and
I want to make sure they're designed to be as fair as
possible to all players. To do this, I need beta testers—
players who play to win while still showing respect
for their fellow players and the game itself.
That's what the grand prize was all about.

After much thought, I've decided that all of the
medalists have exhibited these qualities. That's why
Team Cryptic, Team SuperFan, and Team MADR will **ALL** be
official beta testers for The Masked Medalist LTD!
Keep your eye on this space for more announcements
soon. In the meantime, I hope you enjoy the closing
ceremony. **See you at the next Games . . .**

CHAPTER TWENTY-TWO
MIKA

MIKA CLUNG TO a pole on the crowded train, gazing at a man near the door. He was wearing shorts and a tank top, and every visible inch of skin was covered in yellow, blue, and green body paint—a walking Brazilian flag. Before Mika realized what she was doing, her phone was in her hands and she was moving to get a better angle.

As the train began to slow, the man noticed Mika framing her shot. He gave her a dazzling smile, spreading his arms so she could get the full effect of his paint job. The passengers around him grinned. Just before Mika took the photo, a teenage girl wearing a cat-ears headband and waving a miniature Japanese flag ducked beneath his left arm, flashing a peace sign and beaming.

"Thanks!" Mika called, and the man nodded and smiled. The train came to a halt, and she examined her picture. It was a good shot, even though the lighting wasn't great. But she could adjust that with her photo-editing app. Maybe play with the contrast, too—see if she could balance the blue and green a little better . . .

"Very nice!"

Mika jumped, startled, as she realized Mom and Dad were on either side of her, looking at her phone. She gave them a sheepish grin. "I wasn't going to post it or anything. I just, um . . ."

Mom smiled. "We know. You just saw a good photo opportunity."

"Gavin was right," Dad added, still studying the picture. "You really do have talent."

Mika tried not to look too pleased. The train lurched forward again, and Mom glanced up at the digital map showing their route. "Two more stops, Andy!"

Across the aisle, Andy glanced up from his phone and blinked, looking slightly disoriented. "Oh, okay!"

Mika couldn't help but giggle. The previous night, Hana sent a message to all three teams—MADR, Cryptic, and SuperFan, minus Kaito—about setting up a private chat room so they could discuss the first game she would be sending them next week. Andy had begun playing other puzzle games almost nonstop ever since for practice, texting with Devon and Tyler about the pros and cons of each game.

"You know, we still haven't had a chat about this." Mom tapped Mika's phone, and her smile vanished.

Dad put his arm around Mika's shoulders. "Here's the thing," he said. "We understand why you did it. And honestly? Seeing your picture up on that billboard was really exciting."

"We're so proud of you," Mom added. "But we're disappointed that you didn't tell us about the Enspire contest first."

Mika swallowed. "I figured it wouldn't matter."

"You figured it was better to apologize rather than ask for permission," Dad said, looking amused. "But what's done is done. Mom and I haven't decided exactly what the consequences will be, although you can bet that your chores list is going to get a lot longer for the rest of the summer."

"And the no-social-media-until-you're-thirteen rule still stands." Mom paused. "For personal accounts."

Mika looked up. "Personal accounts?"

"But perhaps we can make an exception for a *professional* account." Dad grabbed the pole as the train slowed again. "Like a photography portfolio."

"On the condition that Dad and I have complete access to the account," Mom added quickly. "You post your photos, but we control the privacy settings, monitor the comments, followers, everything. Okay?"

"Yes!" Mika could hardly believe it. "Thank you!"

"One other thing," Dad said. "If you're really serious about this, we think you should sign up for photography club this fall."

Mika's mouth fell open. "Wait. There's a *photography club?*"

Mom laughed. "There is! We checked the school's website for an extracurriculars list last night. They meet after school every Tuesday. How does that sound?"

"Um, *amazing!*" Mika squeezed her phone, feeling giddy. With all the excitement of traveling to Tokyo for the Olympics, she'd almost forgotten about school starting in a few weeks. When Mika and Riley's fifth-grade class had taken the tour of Marshall Middle School in May, they'd both been intimidated by the whole thing. What if they got lost between classes? What if they couldn't get their lockers open? But if middle school meant that Mika could do cool stuff like an after-school photography club, maybe it wouldn't be so scary after all.

The train slowed again, and Dad nudged Andy with his toe. "This is us!" he said as the doors slid open.

"And everybody else, apparently," Mika said when most of the passengers who'd been sitting got to their feet.

They followed the man in the Brazilian flag body paint off the train, but quickly lost him on the crowded platform. Mika gripped Mom's hand tightly as they made their way to the stairs, Andy and Dad right behind them.

"Did you know Marshall had a photography club?" Mika asked Andy once they'd exited the station.

Andy blinked. "No. But I'm not surprised. There's lots of clubs that meet after school. Book club, astronomy club, chess club . . ."

"There's a book club?!" Mika exclaimed. "Oh wow, I should tell Riley. It'll probably make her feel better."

"Feel better about what?"

"Just . . . middle school," Mika said, shrugging. "We took a tour right before summer break, and it kind of freaked her out. And, well . . . maybe it freaked me out a little bit, too," she admitted.

To her surprise, Andy nodded. "Oh, right—I remember doing that tour in fifth grade! I kept thinking there was no way I'd be able to find all my classes. But it's really not that hard once you get used to it."

"That's what the assistant principal said, but I'm still pretty positive I'm going to get totally lost my first day."

"You definitely won't," Andy said with a grin. "We took the subway in Tokyo by ourselves. We went all over the city and we didn't get lost. Middle school will be easy after this!"

"I didn't even think about that!"

"Besides, if you do need help, you can always ask me," Andy added.

Mika beamed. "Oh, right!"

"Did you forget it's my school, too?" he teased.

"No," Mika said, rolling her eyes. "Well, kind of. I guess I got used to us going to different schools last year."

"Not anymore! We're both in middle school now."

Mika's heart soared as they crossed the street with Mom and Dad, heading toward the stadium. Middle school didn't seem nearly as intimidating.

The crowd seemed to triple in size and sound as a

mass of people slowly made their way into the main arena. Pop music blared from the speakers while some fans danced and jumped around. Mika gasped when she stepped through the double doors.

The arena was dark, with spotlights in different colors soaring over the seats. The track and field had been transformed into a massive white stage that pulsed red every few seconds, like a heartbeat. Mika remembered how incredible the opening ceremony had looked on TV at home. She couldn't believe she was here now, about to see the closing ceremony in person!

"Mika! Andy! Over here!"

Emma jumped up and down, waving her hands over her head. Next to her, Mrs. Botha grinned widely at the Kudos as they made their way to their seats. "Here, we brought extra!" Emma announced, shoving glow sticks into Andy and Mika's hands. "The athletes are already lining up for the Parade of Nations. I told Antony we'd scream his name super loud so he'd be able to see where we're sitting! He begged me not to, which means we *have* to do it."

"Absolutely," Mika said, accepting a glow stick with a laugh.

"Do you think he'll race at the next Olympics?" Andy asked.

Emma nodded. "He wants to, for sure. I hope he does—that means a trip to Paris!"

"Ooh!" Mika wondered if Mom would be covering those Games in four years. Then she remembered something. "Oh, hey—if Antony races in the Summer Games after *that,* you can visit us!"

"Really?"

"Oh, right!" Andy said excitedly. "The 2028 Games are in Los Angeles!"

"Then he definitely has to do it," Emma said, grinning. "Maybe I can even get Tyler to come. And Sabine, too!"

Mika smiled at the thought. Sabine had messaged her, Andy, Emma, and Tyler the previous night and told them that Kaito had apologized to Team SuperFan, and they were all friends again. He was too embarrassed to apologize to the Team MADR and Team Cryptic players . . . *for now,* Sabine had added with a smiley emoji. *But I'll make sure he does soon.*

The illuminated stage suddenly went dark, and Mika felt goose bumps break out on her arms. "It's starting!" she cried, but her words were lost to the deafening sound of fireworks. Everyone looked up to see sparks flying around the opening of Olympic Stadium, rapidly changing from purple, to blue, to red, to green. The *ooh*s and *aah*s were quickly hushed as a low, rhythmic drumbeat began. The stage flared white again, and Mika's heart leapt when at least a hundred dancers appeared seemingly out of thin air. For a brief moment, she felt a pang of sadness as she remembered that this was the closing ceremony—the Olympics, and her trip to Tokyo, were almost over.

Andy nudged her arm. "What's wrong?"

"Oh, nothing," Mika said. "Just kind of sad that it's our last day here."

"Yeah," Andy agreed. "But it's hard to be sad if you think about all the cool *first* days we're about to have!"

"What do you mean?"

"First day of being official beta testers for the Masked Medalist," Andy said. "First day of school."

Mika felt her spirits lift. "First day of photography club. My first professional portfolio."

"Exactly!" Andy exclaimed. "Speaking of photography, don't forget to take pictures of this!"

He pointed to the stage as the dancers were launching into their first routine. Smiling, Mika pulled out her phone. She thought about all of the pictures she'd taken during the trip, and about seeing her photo on that billboard. She thought about all the amazing food they'd eaten, and all the incredible athletes they'd watched. She thought about being co-beta testers with Andy and their friends—the old ones, and the new ones they'd made on this trip.

And suddenly, Mika knew Andy was right. They had no reason to feel sad.

They were ready for another adventure.

ACKNOWLEDGMENTS

We are so proud of this book and grateful to everyone who helped bring the Kudo Kids' first adventure to life. First, we would like to thank our parents for encouraging our love of reading from an early age. It's so exciting that we are now creating stories for a new generation of young readers. We would also like to thank them for teaching us to take care of each other. From early on, this sense of teamwork enabled us to cultivate a special working dynamic between the two of us that has continually motivated us to take on new creative projects.

Theresa Peters, Ty Flynn, and Jonathan Beckerman, thank you for your support and guidance. You believed in our ability to tell a special story and introduced us to the "ball of unlimited energy" who is your colleague, Albert Lee.

Albert, thank you for taking us under your wing. Your enthusiasm is unmatched, and working with you four years after our first meeting has been a wonderful turn of events. You understood why we wanted to go on this journey, and, along with Mary Pender, helped us begin to imagine the amazing adventures the Kudo Kids could have. On top of that, you helped us find the perfect partner in Razorbill, and our editor, Julie Rosenberg.

Julie, you are the editor of our dreams—we couldn't

have done this without you! Your positive attitude and enthusiasm helped us bring our best to every page of the book AND enjoy the process.

Michelle Schusterman, collaborating with you has been an exciting and fulfilling experience. We value your playfulness, curiosity, and passion for storytelling. You are amazing, and we can't wait to continue telling Mika and Andy's story with you.

Yaoyao Ma Van As, thank you for helping us bring the Kudo Kids and Tokyo to life. Your talent, attention to detail, and expressive style adds heart to the book. Locking in the final cover illustration was an electric moment we will always remember.

Alex Sanchez, Casey McIntyre, Jen Klonsky, and Gretchen Durning, thank you for believing in us. Knowing that we have your support is incredibly meaningful. Jayne Ziemba, thank you for your hard work, dedication, and thoroughness.

Maria Fazio and Lindsey Andrews, your creativity and extra effort elevated every design element in the book. Thank you for being so imaginative.

Elyse Marshall, Lindsay Boggs, Naomi Duttweiler, Christina Colangelo, Emily Romero, Alex Garber, Lauren Festa, and Venessa Carson—we really appreciate your passion for this story. All of you have worked ceaselessly to help us share the Kudo Kids with the world—you guys are the best!

Auntie Eva Chen and Edward Barsamian—actually,

the two of you were the first to encourage us to write a book. We listened—thank you!

Jessica Kaye, Stephen George, Karen Dziekonski, and Amber Beard—thank you for helping us bring this book to life in another medium. Recording the audiobook with you was a fun, challenging, and fulfilling experience—we appreciate your patience and encouragement

Justin Antony, Virginia Nam, Jackson Williams, Lauren Schutte, Pamela Chen, and Ashley Yuki, we appreciate your friendship and support.

Marina Zoueva, Massimo Scali, Johnny Johns, Oleg Epstein, and Tina Lundgren, thank you for helping us become the people we are today. We love you all!

Special additional thanks to Janet McDonald, Kathy Bird, Yuki Saegusa, Alissandra Aronow, and Kirk Myers for your faith in us throughout the years.

Finally, to our readers and supporters from all around the world. We are so grateful for the kindness you bring to our lives every day. Your energy inspires us to continue following our dreams. We are always striving to learn, grow, and challenge ourselves with the intention of creating special things that we can share with all of you.